FELINE FATALE

A REX & EDDIE MYSTERY

SEAN CAMERON

DAPPER FOX
PUBLISHING

Cover Photos: Copyright Warren Photography
Cover Design: Anthony S. Hales

ISBN: 1946215015
ISBN-13: 978-1946215017

ONE

Eddie plonked the plastic bag on the office desk. "Say that again? A cat burglar?"

Rex yanked the bag towards him and rummaged through it. "We have a new case. We've got to find a cat burglar."

Rex plucked a veggie wrap from the bag. "What's this?" He scrunched up his face so tight his round, black glasses rolled down his nose.

"It's a wrap." Eddie pulled his rolling chair closer, sat down, and leaned forward. "A cat burglar case? Really?"

Rex glared at the wrap. "What's wrong with sandwiches?"

Eddie rolled his eyes. "We have sandwiches every day, so I grabbed us some wraps. We've been hired to investigate a cat burglar?"

"Veggie wrap? I'm not sure about this, Eddie."

"You like veggies. What did the cat burglar steal?"

"I don't like vegetables. They come from the ground and taste like dirt."

"You like chips."

1

"Chips aren't a vegetable."

"They're potatoes."

Rex flared his nostrils as he poked around the contents of the bag. "I'll eat the crisps."

"Also potatoes," Eddie muttered under his breath. "Tell me what the cat burglar stole."

Rex sat back with his green packet of crisps.

Eddie pointed at the bag. "Cheese and onion? You know an onion is a vegetable."

Rex nodded. "Good point." He dropped the packet back into the bag and picked out another. "I'll eat the barbecue ones instead."

As Rex ate, Eddie grabbed and opened a veggie wrap. "What did the cat burglar steal?"

Rex swallowed. "A cat, obviously."

"That's not a cat burglar. The client is certain the cat was stolen?"

Rex bobbed his head. "Well, we can't rule out the possibility."

"So, you're saying that woman called again about her missing cat?"

He munched and nodded.

Eddie lowered the wrap. "Rex, I'm not interested in working for a cat lady."

"Former cat lady." Rex peered over his glasses. "She's currently without cat."

"Either way, the answer is no."

Rex stuffed a load of crisps in his mouth and bit down with a loud crunch. With his mouth full he said, "You'll have to tell her."

"What's her number?"

"No need to call. She'll be here in a minute. We took the case."

Eddie shook his head. "I have a sinking feeling about this."

"That's your chair, the height adjuster is broken. You said we needed money and to get money, we need a client. Maybe we could spend the profit on a new chair?"

Eddie stared down at his chair. It was so low his knees were raised off the seat. He softened for a second. Rex grinned as he could see Eddie giving in.

Eddie straightened his neck and strengthened his resolve. "Well, that's a waste of time, because we're not gonna take the case."

Rex licked the sprinkles of crisp flavourings off his fingers. "Tell her that then."

Eddie wagged his finger. "You know, Rex. You know I don't like confrontation, that I'm not good at saying no. That's half the reason I'm in this cockeyed organisation with you."

Rex raised his eyebrows.

Eddie stuck out his jaw. "I might not be able to say no, but I'm good at saying yes and not showing up." He bit a chunk out of his wrap. Eddie had plenty more to say, but he hated to talk with his mouth full.

Rex tipped the remains of the packet into his mouth, rolled the bag into a ball, and threw it in the bin, all while Eddie stared.

Eddie swallowed, took in a deep breath, and continued. "So we'll do the little dance. I'll say, 'Milton Miles Investigations, take a seat.' I'll listen and nod as she explains her case, and I'll tell her we'll be in touch. And then, I won't."

Rex feigned a jaw-drop.

"And neither will you," Eddie said. "Because we aren't taking the case. We'll go through all that, but it's your own time you're wasting ... and my time ... and her time, but you're definitely included in the time-wasting. So have fun with that."

"You can't say no to a lady," Rex said.

"To a demented old cat lady, I can."

Someone at the door knocked. Eddie chomped another large lump from his wrap and marched to the door. Rex sat up straight, adjusted his collar, and brushed the fluff from his corduroy jacket. He checked his reflection in the window, licked both his palms, and shaped his scruffy hair.

At the door, Eddie watched Rex groom himself with suspicion. He pulled the door open with an impatient yank. A woman with auburn-red hair and milky-white skin sprinkled in freckles stood in the doorway. Beneath an open grey hoodie, elastic yoga clothes hugged her athletic body. Although the woman was in her late-forties, a healthy workout glow made her look years younger. Her smile lines didn't diminish the sparkle of her grey-blue eyes.

Eddie, almost twenty years younger, found himself distracted by her luminosity. He didn't realise how long they'd stood at the door, until he remembered the lump of veggie wrap on his tongue. Having sat there for far too long, Eddie's gag reflex was likely to kick in any second.

"Milton Miles Investigations?" she asked in a soft voice.

He nodded as he chewed, once again refusing to talk with a mouthful.

"You spy with our little eye," Rex called out from the desk, one eyebrow raised to appear suave.

The woman peered over Eddie's shoulder to see who shouted.

Rex waved. "That's our catchphrase."

"We don't—" Eddie paused, his food not quite finished. He glared at Rex as he swallowed and turned back to the woman with a smile. "We don't have a catchphrase."

"It's a work in progress," Rex offered.

"May I sit?" the woman asked.

"Yes, of course. Take a seat." Eddie gestured to the nicest office chair, which only needed a third of the amount of duct tape to hold the padding together.

As they headed to the desk, Eddie hung back a step so he could sneakily straighten his tie, wipe food crumbs from his chin, and adjust his polyester suit jacket.

Eddie sat in his broken chair and tightened his lips in annoyance. He was shorter than average, and now with the low seat, he looked tiny compared to the six-foot Rex and his standard height chair.

The woman rolled her seat forward to see Eddie better, and her long wavy hair danced along the desk. As she brushed the hair to the side, Eddie felt a hint of recognition. Something about her struck him as familiar.

"How can we help?" Eddie said.

"My name is Beatrice Nerdlinger, and I'm looking for someone to help me find my cat." She placed a photograph of a black cat with a white belly on the desk.

Eddie's eyes stayed on her. "Mrs Nerdlinger? From St Jude's Primary School?"

She nodded.

"I'm Eddie Milton. You taught me and Rex when we were ten."

"Oh, how lovely. And now you're successful detectives?"

Rex gave a proud nod as Eddie winced.

"I still can't believe it," Eddie said. "You can't be Mrs Nerdlinger. You're so…"

Mrs Nerdlinger broke the silence. "I think you were my first class. Eighteen years ago?"

"Yes, Miss." Eddie blushed.

She smiled.

Rex leaned forward. "What's your cat's name, Miss?"

"Nubbin."

Rex raised a corner of his lip.

"Like a stump?" Eddie asked.

"She's missing her tail. Well, most of it. When I took her in a few years ago, someone had run over her tail, and the vet removed it."

"So was she already called Nubbin?" Rex asked.

"Why do you ask?"

"I wondered if it was a nickname given after the accident or not. Like Captain Hook, was he called Hook when he had two hands?"

She gave a polite smile that flashed her pearly teeth. "I don't understand."

"I think Rex is asking if Nubbin was struck by the dramatic irony of having a stump-like name before she lost her tail, or if it was a nickname, you know, for her—"

"Disability?" she said. "That would be pretty insensitive."

Eddie nodded sharply. "Yes of course. That's pretty rude, Rex."

Rex slumped.

"Although, are you sure it's a disability?" Eddie said. "She's not lost her eyesight or legs or anything."

Her false smile faded. "A tail has many functions, including balance."

Rex sighed. "I wish I had a tail."

She smiled at Rex, and he melted. Jealous of the attention, Eddie slapped his hands on the desk to disrupt the moment.

"I think we've got a little off track. What can you tell us about Nubbin?"

"She loves to be petted, and if you stroke under her chin she gives a little purr. It's the only time she makes noise, she's very quiet. Her favourite food is turkey, and she absolutely loves being naked."

Eddie cleared his throat. "Naked?"

She looked Eddie in the eye. "Yes, naked."

"Aren't all cats … naked?"

"Not those that wear collars. She hated having a collar, always made a fuss until I took it off."

Rex examined the photo. "When did you last see Nubbin?"

"She's been gone for two weeks now. She usually comes and goes, but she's never gone more than a few days. I've been to the local vet to ask if anyone handed her in, but no luck."

"Any suspicions?" Rex said. "Could she have been cat-burgled?"

"Stolen," Eddie said.

Rex's eyes widened. "Catnapped?"

"Quiet, Rex."

Mrs Nerdlinger zipped up her hoodie and stuffed her hands into the pockets. "I hate to think someone would steal a cat, but it may be a possibility."

Eddie bit his bottom lip. "Because?"

"Because I only wear sandals, but the day she went missing it rained hard, and I found thick, large boot prints in the back garden."

"You don't know anyone else that could have made those prints. Any guests?"

"Absolutely not," she snapped. It was an odd shift in tone.

Eddie bobbed his head. "It's not a lot to go on."

"We'll take the case, though. Right, Eddie?"

"It's not really the type of work we're…" He hesitated.

As Mrs Nerdlinger waited for his response, a single tear dropped from her eye. The tear slowed at the top edge of her left cheekbone and dropping down her heart-shaped face.

Eddie swallowed. "I mean, well, we can pop around and take a look. Rex and I can then assess the situation further."

She smiled, and her whole face glowed. When she wasn't looking, Eddie gave Rex a hard stare. Rex grinned back.

TWO

Eddie parked the Morris Minor outside the address Beatrice Nerdlinger gave them, 47B Parade Lane. After he turned off the engine, he pulled the handbrake up. The car still crept down the slight slope of the street. Using both hands, he tugged the handbrake a few extra clicks. Rex and Eddie sat still as the rocking car settled. The Morris Minor stayed in place. Eddie gave a firm nod, and the pair got out of the car.

The old 1971 Morris Minor 1000 Traveller had seen better days. In over forty years, the lime-green paint had faded from what little sun England had to offer. Although they'd spent money on a few repairs, the duo saved some cash by replacing a missing wing mirror with a glued-on bathroom shaving mirror.

At Mrs Nerdlinger's address, a red brick driveway led from the pavement towards the centre of two bungalows and split off to each front door. The two properties were bordered by the same foot-high brick wall.

Both homes received various renovations. The left

house had white walls with minimalist window frames and angular drainage systems all in bright white plastic. On the right, Beatrice Nerdlinger's home had a heavy wooden door, warped glass panel windows, and the original curvy gutters. Trinkets and thirsty potted plants lined the patio.

The Nerdlinger house had a quaint charm thanks to its lived-in aesthetic and a choir of croaking frogs emanating from the garden pond.

Eddie reached his finger towards the doorbell when Rex pushed his hand to the side and pressed the button. Eddie straightened his suit jacket as they waited.

Rex pressed his face to the front room's warped glass window, but the drawn curtains blocked his view. He shrugged. "She's not home?" Rex knelt on the moss-lined uneven patio slabs around the pond.

Eddie checked the clock on his phone. "We're on time. If she's not here in five minutes, we drop the case."

"We can't do that to Mrs Nerdlinger."

"Yes we can, we haven't taken the case yet."

"But you love her."

Eddie sneered. "I do not love her. You love her. I saw you tidy yourself up before she came into the office."

Rex shrugged. "Fine, we both love her."

"I do not love her."

"But you wrote her a handmade love letter for Valentine's Day?"

Eddie scoffed. "What? When?"

"In class."

"When I was ten?"

"Yeah."

"You are loving this, aren't you. I'm not interested in chasing after a missing cat so you can be teacher's pet."

"Nubbin is already teacher's pet." Rex offered his hand

to a tiny frog by the pond. It crept onto his palm. "Don't you want to find out what happened to the cat?"

Eddie sighed. "Sort of. Part of me is a little worried that this cat thief is insane. I don't want to go up against some psycho that turns cats into lampshades."

Rex stood back up and examined the tiny frog in his hand. "You're such a cynic."

"What are we gonna say? The good news is we found your cat, the bad news is your cat's been turned into a lampshade? How do you turn that into a positive?"

Rex shrugged. "Give her the lampshade? She'd be the rightful owner."

"Perfect," Eddie said sarcastically.

Rex poked the tiny frog with his finger. "What's a baby frog called?"

"A tadpole?"

"No, after tadpole."

"I think they go from frogspawn to tadpole to frog."

"But a baby frog should have a name."

"Tadpoles do have names. I'm pretty sure they're adults as frogs. Teenagers, minimum."

"This is a baby frog." Rex offered his hand so Eddie could see the frog.

"Get that thing away from me." Eddie stumbled on a tuft of grass as he backed away.

Rex stepped towards Eddie. "You don't like frogs."

Eddie cocked his head back. "I don't like green, slimy things."

Rex pulled the frog back and placed his spare hand over the little creature to cover his ears from the insult. "He's not slimy. He's shiny."

"Are you boys in need of some assistance?" A nasal voice asked.

Both turned to the neighbour's front garden. A tall man in his late forties with greased-back hair and a greying moustache sneered at the detectives.

He held his arms at his hips. "Do you care to tell me who you are, and why you're sneaking about on the property of my neighbour?"

"She's a client," Rex said.

"Shush." Eddie leaned in for a whisper. "He might be a suspect, we can't give away our status."

"A client? And what pray tell is your business? You're not masseuses are you?"

"No," Rex said. "We're detec—"

"Decorators," Eddie said. "We do wallpaper and painting. She saw us work on a nearby house and asked us to spruce the place up."

"Beatrice? Decorate? Chance would be a fine thing. She hasn't decorated since I've known her."

"Are you two close?" Eddie asked.

"I should think so since I live next door to her. Can't get much closer than that."

"No, I mean do you know her well?"

"Very well," he said with a pencil-thin smile that sent a shiver down Eddie's neck.

"Like dating and stuff?" Rex asked.

Eddie rolled his eyes at Rex's inability to recognise subtlety.

"That's how it started." The man's smile broke open to reveal his thin, yellowed teeth.

"Did it end when you made that face?" Eddie said.

The man's smile dropped, exposing his snaggletoothed bottom row. "It ended when she went nuts. That woman is a basket-case. Don't say you haven't been forewarned." His eyes looked the pair up and down. "Where's your paint gear then? Or are you going to paint in a suit?"

Eddie gave an awkward smile as he waited for inspiration. "We're here … to price up the work." He reached out his arms to highlight the suit. "Got to make a good first impression."

The man stepped onto the central driveway and cocked his head. "Didn't she meet you when she saw you work?"

"Right…" Eddie hesitated, struggling to add to his story. "Yes, you didn't let me finish. Got to make a good first impression, and you've got to make a good second impression as well. That's company policy."

The man's eyes glazed over, indicating Eddie bored him enough to dim his suspicions.

"Well, we'd best get on." Eddie waved.

"Goodbye." The man folded his arms and continued to watch.

Eddie stomped to the front door and gave a solid, loud knock.

The man leaned his weight on one leg. "She's not home."

"How do you know?" Rex asked.

"I know because I've got eyes," the man said in frustration. He pointed to his front window. "That's my office. I see everything that goes on here, and she hasn't come home yet."

"You work from home?" Eddie said.

"Yes, I buy and sell stocks."

"That's cool," Rex said.

"It's stressful. You couldn't do it, either of you. I've suffered three heart attacks. That said, I did earn a fortune."

"Then why don't you avoid the stress and quit?" Eddie said.

"Because I lost a fortune, didn't I? Up, down, up,

13

down. A lot of down the last five years, but we shall endure. Ian Stork is the name. Stork by name, Stock by nature."

Rex smiled at the novelty. "Stock is your name and your trade?"

"No, Stork is my name. Stock is my trade."

Eddie shook his head. "That's not how you use the saying."

"Of course it is. I said it, didn't I?"

Eddie stepped forward. "So you see a lot of what goes on around here?"

"I saw you."

"Did you see a cat? A black cat without a tail."

"A bit of tail," Rex said. "A nubbin."

"Nubbin by name, nubbin by nature," Eddie said. "That's how you use the saying."

Stork narrowed his eyes at Eddie. "I've seen plenty of cats around here. The filthy frog pond attracts them, and I end up with a garden full of cat turds." He pointed to Beatrice Nerdlinger's house and shook his finger with each word. "She's a cat lady in waiting, if she's not a full-blown cat lady by now. You know, cats carry a parasite transferable to humans."

Eddie grimaced. "I don't think I want to know about this."

"Toxoplasma gondii, it's called. It can only breed in cats, so it makes its rat or mouse host do things to end up getting eaten."

"Sounds pretty harmless to humans then," Eddie said.

"It makes female mice interested in cats, so they walk right up to the cat and get eaten."

"The cat attracts its prey," Rex said with a grin. "Like a femme fatale?"

Stork sneered. "Human women do the same, they cosy right up to the little blighters."

Eddie shrugged. "Well, they're not gonna get eaten, so I think it's fine."

"Now, men. When the male rodent has the parasite, it becomes impulsive and takes more risks, gives away its position, which gives the cat a hunting advantage. Does the same thing to men!"

"Again, I'm not gonna get hunted by a cat, so I fail to see your point."

"It makes a man take all sorts of risks, it could ruin your life."

Eddie gulped; that did sound nasty.

"Is that why you lose money on the stock exchange?" Rex innocently asked. "Because you take more risks?"

Stork turned a shade of white, he'd apparently never thought of this before.

"It's a bad market," he mumbled.

A ginger cat walked on the brick wall along Stork's garden. He stomped at it and waved his arms. The cat ran, leapt across the driveway, and rubbed itself against Rex's leg.

"Why she loves those furry little monsters, I don't know."

Rex bent down to stroke the feline. "I like cats."

Stork scolded Rex. "Then you're a lucky fool. She's got three or four, but she'd have plenty more if they didn't meet such unfortunate ends."

Eddie rubbed his chin. "She lost other cats?"

"Over the years. She had a grey cat for a while, horrible little bugger it was, and it disappeared. Another was run over in the street. Then Nubbin had its tail run over. Any cat owned by her should be listed as an endangered animal."

"Well, thanks for your time," Eddie said, hoping to clear him away.

As Stork walked back to his house, he pointed to his eyes and back at the detectives.

Eddie turned to Rex. "Two dead or missing cats. You think the cats are all connected?"

Rex raised an eyebrow. "Well, they're all owned by Mrs Nerdlinger."

"I mean I think someone's got it in for these cats. Right now, Ian Stork is the most likely suspect."

Rex smiled. "We should take him down and impress Mrs Nerdlinger?"

"You mean get *paid* by Mrs Nerdlinger."

"Of course." Rex avoided eye contact.

"This is a paid case."

Rex focused on the pond. "Yeah."

"Look at me and say this is a paid case."

He turned to Eddie and winced. "This is a paid case?"

Eddie bared his teeth. "So it's not. You said it like it's a question. Like I forced you to say it."

"You *did* force me to say it."

Eddie stepped towards Rex, who raised his palm using the frog as protection.

"Fine," Eddie said. "What happened?"

"On the phone she asked if we do pro-bono cases."

"And you said yes."

"Only because I didn't know what pro-bono meant."

Eddie waved his arms. "Oh well, *that's* okay then."

Rex sunk his head. "When I looked it up and saw it meant free, I knew you'd be angry. I thought it was a legal term, like class action, or injunction, or after David."

"Affidavit?" Eddie asked.

"Yeah, that's what I said."

"That's not what you said. You said after David."

Rex gave an exasperated huff. "That's what you said? Why do we keep saying after David?"

"We're not. I'm saying affidavit. It's one word. What do you think it means?"

Rex thought it over. "It's when a statement is written down and used as evidence."

Eddie sighed relief.

"Because," Rex began, "David checked it over and agreed to it."

Eddie's shoulders hunched up. "And who exactly is David?"

"I don't know. I never needed an after David?"

"Affidavit!" Eddie screamed through gritted teeth. "So what did you think pro-bono was? Being a fan of U2?"

Rex avoided eye contact and peered at his shoes.

Eddie stomped down the driveway. "No free cases. No pro-bono."

"You're leaving?"

He spun around. "No. We're gonna crack the case."

Rex smiled. "Because it's the professional thing to do?"

"No."

"Because you love Mrs Nerdlinger and want to make her happy?"

"No." Eddie stomped up to Rex to talk privately. "Because I want to prove Ian Stork took the cat."

"For justice?"

"Because I don't like him."

Rex put his arm around Eddie. "That's the spirit."

Eddie cringed at the arm squeeze and pulled Rex's hand off him one finger at a time. Rex side-stepped to give Eddie back his personal space.

The frog jumped from Rex's hand and landed at Eddie's foot. Eddie bounced back and fell on the pavement. The frog hopped back into the pond.

As Eddie lay on the ground, Rex leaned into Eddie's view and smiled.

"Here comes Mrs Nerdlinger. You best get up. We want to make a good second impression, remember. That's our motto."

Eddie strained. "You know that's not our motto, right?"

THREE

Beatrice Nerdlinger stood over Eddie as he got up from the grassy ground and brushed away the loose, green blades. She wore a casual, draped-off-the-shoulder green dress that ended below the knees. Her arms were toned, not overly muscular but she could probably take either of them in a fight. From the ground, Eddie admired her tiny ankles. As she folded her arms, Eddie decided second impressions were indeed important.

"Hello boys, what are you doing down there?"

"Detecting?" Eddie offered.

Rex nodded. "He's trying to get a cat's point of view."

Eddie gave a smile, unsure if she'd bought their story.

Beatrice Nerdlinger cocked her head. "How ... thorough."

At the patio, Beatrice Nerdlinger grabbed a box of cat food from under a bench. She showered the dry fodder all over the concrete as five cats appeared from various hedges and ate.

Rex stroked a cat as it noisily chewed. "You have five cats? Your neighbour said you had three."

"Well, I'd say five, but I guess two of them are more like guests that recently showed up. Ian would know. He's always on the lookout."

Rex frowned. "He's mean."

She nodded. "Yes, he is. Allergic to cats, apparently, and quite bitter about the whole thing."

"But you two get on, right?" Eddie said. "I mean, you both worked together on the garden?"

"Oh, Ian did that himself. He asked if he could do some landscaping. I said as long as the pond wasn't touched, he could help himself. When I came back after the summer holidays, he'd installed a driveway and walls."

Rex gestured to the front door. "Can we come in?"

"Oh no. That won't be necessary."

Eddie gave an apologetic smile. "Well, a full search is part of the investigation."

"No," she said.

Rex and Eddie looked at each other in confusion.

"We'd like to check out Nubbin's surroundings," Eddie said. "So we can spot a clue or two?"

"I don't entertain guests. What kind of clues are you looking for? Maybe I can help."

"It's more of a look-around-and-feel-inspired-by-stuff situation."

Beatrice Nerdlinger stroked a cat that cuddled up to her ankle. "I don't see why that's necessary, Nubbin obviously isn't in the house. It's the last place you need to look."

Rex glanced over the fence. "Can we have a peek around the back garden?"

"She's not there either."

"But the shoe print is," Eddie said. "We need to check that out."

She raised her eyebrows. "Just the outside?"

The pair nodded.

"Okay."

She scattered more cat food along the concrete while Rex and Eddie stepped through the side gate into the back garden. The flower beds were covered with crowded weeds while the lawn was overgrown with dry mud patches.

At a window, Eddie tried to look through the crack in the drawn curtains, but the lights were off. Not a single window let in any light. Eddie turned to Rex, who examined a birdhouse covered in dry-rot. He waved Rex over to the back door.

Rex stopped a few feet short of the door. "That's it." He pointed at a solid boot-print directed away from the door, stamped in the now-dry and crusty ground.

Eddie kneeled to get a closer look. "It did rain pretty hard two weeks ago. Same time as Nubbin disappeared."

Rex followed the direction of the boot "The suspect headed towards Ian Stork's fence."

"To the back corner of his garden?" Eddie said. "But, why?"

Rex jumped to view over the fence. "He has a shed."

Eddie turned to Beatrice Nerdlinger's back door. "Why won't she let us in?"

"I don't know, but it makes me want to go in more."

The pair quietly approached the back door. Eddie tried to turn the handle, but the door was locked.

Defeated, they stepped back as Rex's foot slid. He lifted up his leg, a layer of brown mush had smeared along the sole.

"Ugh, cat poo."

Eddie raised his hands in a panic. "All right, watch your step."

Rex scraped his foot against a plant pot. From the corner of his eye, he noticed the back door had a cat flap. He cocked his head.

"Should I check it out?"

Eddie nodded. "Be my guest."

Rex pushed the flap in and poked his head inside. The floor tiles confirmed this was the kitchen, but drapes and curtains blocked the light so he couldn't make out details. He pulled his head out of the cat flap.

"I can't see anything?"

Eddie pulled Rex back. "Let me look."

Through the cat flap, Eddie could see the vague shape of furnishings, but it was too dark. He pulled one hand in and put it on the ground to better support his weight. The floor felt coarse and crunchy, not like tiles at all.

The light from the open cat flap revealed Eddie's hand in a cat litter tray, with cat turds scattered all over the surface.

"Ahh!" Eddie pulled back, screaming at his hand as he crawled across the garden.

"What's wrong?" Rex grabbed Eddie's hand and checked for an injury.

"Crap!" Eddie said.

He whipped his hand from Rex and rubbed it in the tall grass to clean himself. His hand brushed against a fresh cat poo. Eddie jumped up straight and whimpered. Poo, and possibly the dreaded toxoplasma gondii parasite, surrounded them.

"What's the matter?"

"Crap. Actual crap. The parasite. I put my hand in cat poo."

Rex scrunched up his face and wiped his hands on his trousers. "Why'd you let me touch you?"

"I didn't let you, you grabbed me."

"Out of concern, you should've warned me."

"I did. I shouted crap."

A deep, bellowing laugh came from inside the house

next door. The pair turned to Ian Stork's home. Over the fence and through a window, the forehead and smiling eyes of the man bobbed with a chuckle. Eddie flared his nostrils at Stork and stomped back around to the front garden. Rex followed and found Mrs Nerdlinger sat on the patio bench scratching a cat behind the ear. Both detectives stared at the cat with envious eyes.

"Sorry to keep you," Eddie said.

"It's no trouble. I'm happy snuggling up with my kitties."

Rex leaned to Eddie's ear and whispered. "Isn't that the female symptom of the parasite?"

"Shut up," Eddie muttered.

"So, any leads?" Mrs Nerdlinger asked.

Eddie shook his head. "Not really, Miss."

She looked off into the distance, distressed but too embarrassed to look at the pair. "That is a shame."

Eddie turned to Stork's house where Stork watched from his living room window. The nosey neighbour grinned and folded his arms. He turned back to Mrs Nerdlinger. "Although, we do have an idea. A sort of half-lead. Do you think he might be involved in the disappear-ance of Nubbin?"

"Ian? No, he's all bark and no bite. He does resent the cats, though."

Rex scratched his head. "Miss, do your cats eat rats?"

"Don't answer that question!" Eddie said.

"Rats? No."

Rex patted Eddie on the shoulder; they were in the clear.

"They usually gift me with frogs or birds ... oh, and mice."

Eddie slumped. "Perfect."

"Anything else?"

Rex raised a hand. "Yes, Miss. What's a baby frog called? After it's been a tadpole?"

"Good question, Rex. Why don't you look it up and tell the rest of us."

Rex nodded. "Okay, Miss."

———————

Later in the evening, Eddie drove with Rex back to Ian Stork's house. To keep a safe distance, Eddie parked across the street a few houses away and watched through binoculars. The evening went fine until Ian Stork pulled a chair up to the living room window, sat with a cup of tea, and stared back at the pair.

The detectives sat in silence watching the man sip his tea for ten minutes.

Rex tapped his fingers on the interior of the car door. Tap, tap, tap. Tap, tap, tap.

"Rex, will you cut that out?"

"I'm bored. Let's call it a night."

Eddie nodded at Stork. "The suspect is in sight. We're on a stakeout."

"But he can see us."

"We'll watch him all night if we have to."

Rex slumped into his seat. "It's seven pm."

Eddie's pettiness had compromised the case, and he knew it, but he couldn't back down now. "I suppose he's not gonna incriminate himself while he can see us, but if we leave now, he wins."

Rex screwed up his eyebrows. "He wins a staring competition?"

"This is a standoff," Eddie said.

Rex sighed and looked at Mrs Nerdlinger's home. "Where is she?"

24

"Mrs Nerdlinger? I'm sure she's home."

"None of her lights are on. I think she fed the cats and left." Rex grimaced at Eddie. "Who does that?"

"Someone with a prior engagement?"

"I'm going for a walk." Rex put his smile back on. "Do you have any money?"

Eddie narrowed his eyes. "Walking is free."

"I was gonna go to the corner shop for food."

"You already ate a bag of snacks."

"I can't walk around aimlessly, I need a task. I only want a fiver."

Eddie opened his wallet. "I've only got a tenner."

"That'll do." Rex yanked the note out of the wallet and opened the passenger door.

"I want change, and a receipt for expenses."

Rex nodded and left.

Eddie turned to Stork. After a few minutes, Stork raised his drink and smiled, as if to toast him. Eddie shook his head. He raised his bottle of Fanta and attempted a smile. Not taking his eyes off Stork, lifted the drink to his mouth and missed. The sticky, orange liquid streamed down his front.

Stork howled with laughter, stood, and pulled his blinds closed while shaking his head.

A knock at the window startled Eddie. Rex had returned.

"The door's unlocked," Eddie said.

Rex sat in his seat.

"You got change?"

Rex smiled. "I got red vines." He dropped a large tub of red vines on Eddie's lap. "Those are for sharing, Eddie. So don't eat them all."

"And my change?"

"These are your snacks too."

25

"So, no change?"

Rex placed one pound and ten pence in Eddie's palm.

"How much did this cost?"

"I ate the rest on the way back."

"You were only gone for a minute."

"Because I ran back after I found this."

Rex pulled a piece of paper from his pocket and handed it to Eddie. He unfolded the ruffled paper, revealing a missing cat poster. The cat was black with a white belly and resembled Nubbin. Below the picture, a reward of fifty pounds was offered for the cat's return.

"Mrs Nerdlinger is offering a reward," Rex said. "Yet she wants us to work for free. What's that all about?"

Eddie studied this paper. "This isn't Mrs Nerdlinger's poster."

Rex pointed his finger at the photo. "But that's a picture of Nubbin."

Eddie nodded. "This cat is a lot like Nubbin, but the poster says the cat's name is Cleopatra."

"Maybe that was her name before she lost the tail."

"But Mrs Nerdlinger didn't tell us that." Eddie straightened his spine. "In fact, she wouldn't tell us Nubbin's old name. What is she up to?"

Eddie dialled the number. "Hello, Mrs Nerdlinger?"

"Wrong number," a hoarse, female voice answered.

"No actually, I'm calling about your cat."

"My cat? You found Cleopatra?"

"Not exactly, but I have some information. Can we meet?"

"Where would you like to meet?"

Rex sat up in excitement. "The multi-storey car park by Tesco."

Eddie shook his head and waved at Rex as if he was a bad smell. Rex sat back, defeated.

"Your house will be fine." Eddie wrote down the address. "I'll see you soon." He hung up.

"Why not the car park? That's where people do information exchanges."

"Because we're not giving her government secrets. We're asking her about her missing cat."

FOUR

R ex and Eddie skimmed through a row of terrace houses, searching for the door number. Each house was thin with overly large concrete window sills. At 36 Border Road, a small concrete slab served as a front garden. The detective duo stepped the whole two-feet from the street to the front door. Eddie reached for the door knocker, but Rex grabbed it and bashed with enthusiasm.

The door opened, revealing a long hallway that faded into darkness. A small old lady with grey curls and thick glasses stood before them.

"Mrs Pickles?"

"Yes."

"I'm Eddie Miles, we spoke on the phone about Cleopatra the cat."

"Oh, yes." She turned to Rex and sneered like she wasn't expecting a second person.

"I'm Rex Milton, his partner."

"Business partner. We're detectives. Can we come inside?"

She shrugged her shoulders and tottered down the hallway. She took a sharp right into the living room. Rex and Eddie took the open door as an invitation and followed.

In the living room, the pair sat down on an old two-piece sofa. Three-piece sofas seemed to be the standard this century, so the duo uncomfortably bumped elbows. On Eddie's side, he inspected cat scratches up the sofa leg.

Mrs Pickles handed over a hefty photo album. "This is my Cleopatra."

Eddie examined the photos. All of them showed the cat without a tail.

He compared the pictures of Cleopatra to the photo Mrs Nerdlinger gave them of Nubbin. It was the same cat. Black fur with a white belly and a nub of a tail.

"What's Cleopatra like?" Rex asked.

Mrs Pickles smiled for the first time, showing off a set of perfect false teeth. "She loves being stroked, especially under her chin. She's very quiet, and she hates wearing a collar."

"And her favourite food is turkey?" Rex said.

She lowered her eyebrows, which dipped in her large, thick lenses at double the size. "How'd you know that?"

Eddie winced. "Does she disappear for several days at a time?"

"She does, but not for weeks like this. How do you know all this?"

"Because she's Mrs Nerdlinger's cat," Rex said.

"No, no. She was a stray cat," Mrs Pickles said. "I rescued her many years ago."

Eddie leaned forward, as much as the poorly sprung couch would let him. "Do you remember when you got her?"

"Years ago. Why?"

Eddie bared his bottom teeth. "Well, someone else is claiming ownership of your cat."

Rex nodded.

"You found the thief?"

Eddie shook his head. "No."

Mrs Pickles dismissed them with a wave of her arms. "What are you talking about then?"

"We were originally hired to find Nubbin ... uh, Cleopatra ... by a different person. It seems the cat has two owners."

"So she kidnapped my cat?"

"No, she's lost the cat, too."

"That woman kidnapped my Cleopatra when she held her against her will."

Eddie's forehead crinkled. "You're accusing Mrs Nerdlinger of kidnapping your cat, on a twice-weekly basis, for the last few years?"

"Exactly."

"Leaving no ransom note, and allowing the cat to leave whenever it wants?"

She folded her arms. "What are you getting at?"

"I'm saying your cat has two owners."

"One owner, and some hussy!" Her rage calmed. "Sorry, dears. Cup of tea?"

Both shook their heads, a little taken aback by the outburst.

"If you find Cleopatra, you're to bring her to me. How much is this hussy paying you? I'll double it."

"Nothing," Rex said.

"Let's see, double nothing..." Mrs Pickles screwed up her face. "I'm not as good at maths as I used to be, what would that be, dear?"

Eddie bobbed his head. "Two hundred?"

Rex's jaw dropped. He nudged Eddie to make sure his full shock was registered. Eddie sneered and elbowed him back.

"Two hundred pounds?" Mrs Pickles said, shocked. "Well, I … uh, I suppose…"

Eddie glanced at the reward poster, which said fifty pounds.

"We'll do it for a hundred," Eddie said.

Rex lowered back in his seat, only minimally outraged.

Mrs Pickles gave a broad smile, which seemed small compared to her bulbous glasses. "Oh, yes. That's nice of you."

"Providing you're the rightful owner," Eddie said.

"What's that supposed to mean?" Mrs Pickles said, rising back to her previous rage.

"You're the second person to claim the cat. We need to be sure that we're returning Cleopatra to the right person."

"Fine, two hundred." She reclined into her easy chair and stared at the pair.

Eddie bit his lip. "It's not about the money, it's about giving the cat to the rightful owner."

"Then give her to me."

As she rolled her eyes, her convex specs warped her irises in shape and size, which made the pair cringe. Rex squirmed involuntarily towards Eddie, thanks to the short sofa they almost butted heads.

"She does know the cat's real name," Rex offered. "The one before the accident."

Eddie turned back to Mrs Pickles and smiled. "So did you know Cleopatra when she had a tail."

"Of course I did!" she snapped. "She's my cat."

"So how'd she lose the tail?"

She scoffed. "I don't know."

"Did you take her to the vet about it?"

"No, she went out for a couple of days, like she does, and came back with the short tail and stitches. The stitches were gone later."

"And you didn't question it?"

"She's a cat, how's she going to answer questions?"

Rex nodded. "Fair point."

"I mean," Eddie clicked his jaw. "You didn't think maybe she had another owner?"

"I'm the owner. How many times do I need to say it?"

Rex sat up, excited like he had an idea. "Do you have a birth certificate?"

Mrs Pickles crinkled her nose. "No, I don't."

He thought for a second. "Why not?"

Exasperated, Eddie threw his hands in the air. "Because it's a bloody cat."

"Because I adopted her."

"From a rescue centre?" Rex asked. "Which one?"

Mrs Pickles took off her glasses and wiped the lenses with a cloth. "I rescued her from the street."

Eddie turned to Rex to whisper. "So we have two clients, both claiming ownership of the same missing cat, and both found her on the street. There's no paper trail."

Rex sighed, "What are we meant to do?"

Mrs Pickles held the thick frames of her glasses to her mouth and exhaled.

"You give me back my cat," her giant mouth said.

"We'll be in touch," Eddie replied.

With a sharp turn, Eddie drove the Morris Minor into Parade Lane and parked close to Mrs Nerdlinger's home. As the pair approached her house, the blinds of Ian Stork's windows fluttered. They were being watched. Rex knocked on her front door, and the duo waited.

The sound of a bolt unlocking sent Rex and Eddie's attention towards the fence gate at the side of the house.

The gate creaked opened enough to get a peek at the pair. After a pause, Mrs Nerdlinger opened the gate wide and joined them on the patio. She wore a long, dangly, white dress decorated with a white lace pattern. The sun shone through the dress's loose edges outlining a silhouette of her svelte figure.

"Hello, boys. Have you found Nubbin?"

As she brushed her long hair back, a sleeve slipped away from the wide neckline and down her shoulder, revealing a cream-coloured bra-strap.

"No, Miss. Not yet." Eddie looked away and pointed at her bare shoulder.

"Excuse me." She pulled the sleeve back in place.

"We have a, uh," Eddie cleared his throat, "complication."

"Oh dear, that doesn't sound good."

Rex handed her Mrs Pickles's reward poster.

Eddie pointed at the piece of paper. "This woman claims Nubbin is her cat, and she's put out a reward for her return."

Rex counted the three cats eating dry food off the patio. "You've got less cats?"

"Fewer cats," she said as she reviewed the poster. "They come and go."

"Mrs Pickles named her Cleopatra," Eddie said. "She looks after Nubbin during the days she goes missing."

Eddie handed over the photos of Mrs Pickles and Cleopatra snuggling up. Mrs Nerdlinger's eyes glazed over as she shook her head.

"That monster stole my cat."

"Mrs Pickles claims to have owned the cat before she lost the tail, but doesn't have proof. We can't work out who stole the cat from who."

Mrs Nerdlinger scoffed. "I did not steal my own cat."

"I'm not saying … it's a poor choice of words. Not that either of you stole the cat."

Her lips tensed. "She did."

Ian Stork opened his side-gate and dragged a heavy, metal bin into the front garden. Rex and Eddie stared as he carried it to the street.

"Afternoon, Beatrice," he said.

"Hello, Ian. This is Rex Milton and Eddie Miles, they're my detect—"

"Decorators," Eddie shouted.

"Right," Ian said. "We've met."

He placed the bin on the pavement and trekked back across the garden into his house. No one spoke as he passed. "Don't mind me, I'm not going to steal your paint colour ideas."

As soon as Stork closed his front door, Eddie got back to business.

"Please, Mrs Nerdlinger, can you tell us when you first got Nubbin?"

"It was a couple of years ago, maybe three. My first cat, Professor Buttons, he died and I … well, I made my home available to all cats. I wanted to make sure all cats were cared for."

Rex kept his narrowed eyes on Ian Stork's bin. "What happened to Professor Buttons?"

"He went missing, and I put up posters. A lady called me. She'd taken a poorly street cat that met my description to a vet. She said the vet suggested he be put down, so she agreed. I went in, and I identified the cat."

"They make you do that for cats?" Rex asked.

"No, I insisted. I wanted to say goodbye to that beautiful, fluffy, grey tabby one last time."

Eddie gave a sympathetic nod. "So how did Cleopatra … uh, Nubbin … come into your life?"

"I fed a neighbourhood cat, and she visited regularly. When her tail was run over, I remembered Professor Buttons being taken to the vet by a stranger. I took Nubbin to the vet to make sure she was taken care of. I paid for everything to make sure she survived. I treated her wound, and we became the best of friends."

Rex scratched his head. "So she was kind of your cat before she lost the tail. It's a tie."

Mrs Nerdlinger handed the photos back. "What are you going to do?"

Eddie stared at the reward money on Mrs Pickles's poster. "Mrs Pickles offered us two hundred pounds," he muttered.

"What was that, Eddie?" Mrs Nerdlinger said. "Speak so the rest of us can hear."

"Nothing, Miss."

Rex shrugged. "I guess we should find the cat first and work it out from there. Right, Eddie?"

"Um, yeah, of course. I think we'll do what Rex says."

Rex smiled. "Really? We're gonna do what I said?"

Eddie winced as he half-shrugged, half-nodded. "Yeah."

"Great!" Rex's spine straightened, and he grew an inch taller with pride. "Let's check Ian Stork's bin."

Rex marched across the garden.

Eddie followed. "Rex, wait."

"Not all the cats are here," Rex said. "I think Stork is killing them."

"We can't do this, not in broad daylight."

As soon as they crossed over into Stork's side of the driveway, his front door opened.

"Get off my property!" Stork barked.

"In a minute," Rex said.

"We're just leaving," Eddie said.

Stork ran across the garden to cut them off.

Rex grabbed the metal bin lid; Stork snatched it back and closed the bin.

"Get off, now. Or I'll call the police."

Stork dragged his bin back across the garden as Rex tried to grab at it.

Eddie bit his lip as he watched Stork head towards the side gate.

What's he hiding? Eddie wondered.

He nodded at Rex. The pair ran after Stork and tried to grab the bin. Stork sprinted to the gate and shoved the bin into his back garden. He slammed the gate behind him.

"Get off my property!"

Eddie turned to Rex. "That was weird."

"Very weird," Mrs Nerdlinger said from her patio, glaring at the pair.

Both muttered in unison, "Sorry, Miss."

FIVE

At ten pm, Eddie parked the car down the street from Stork's home. He and Rex snuck through an alleyway that ran behind the houses on Parade Lane. They counted the houses until they reached the tall wooden fence of Ian Stork's back garden.

Rex jumped so he could peek over the fence. "All the lights are off. I think he's gone to bed."

"Let's do this," Eddie said.

Rex grabbed the top of the fence and Eddie pushed him up.

His legs flailed all over Eddie's shoulders and head before he managed to flip himself over the top of the fence.

Eddie clung to the top of the fence and attempted to lift himself. He used the alleyway's opposite wall to kick from and got his head and arms over the top. His legs lost all grip and hung with the top of the fence wedged up into his armpits.

"I'll help," Rex said.

"No," Eddie whispered, partly to avoid making noise

and partly out of general exhaustion.

Rex either didn't hear or didn't pay attention. He grabbed both of Eddie's hands and pulled with his full weight.

Eddie groaned as Rex tried to pull him over the fence, but instead tugged him into it. Rex let go and scratched his head. Eddie used his remaining strength to crawl one arm back into the alley and pushed himself away from the fence. He fell back to the bumpy, cold alleyway.

In the darkness, Eddie's imagination got the better of him. He swore the fence swayed forward and back, as if the vines wrapped around the wood panels had come to life. After a loud crack, a section of the fence pulled away into the dark. Two fists punched through the vines and ripped away the dried and dead plant.

Rex's head popped through the hole and smiled. "It was a little hard to open, but I found a fence door."

As Eddie stood, Rex kicked through the foliage until he'd made a hole as big as the door. Eddie stepped over the branches and through the gate. Nothing but the moon and stars lit the garden.

"He's got the cat," Rex said.

"How'd you know?"

"Evidence." Rex pointed to faeces by their feet. "Who has cat poo in their garden but no cat?"

"The neighbour of a cat lady? Cats go where they want. Now be careful not to touch anything, we don't want the parasite, remember?"

Rex pulled his chin in. "Right. Although on the bright side, you can't catch it twice, right?"

"We don't … We can't…" Eddie's entire head itched thinking of his brain being home to a parasite. "Just don't talk about it, okay?"

Eddie's feet dragged through the long grass as he

stepped closer to the house. He stopped. Everything about Ian Stork's front garden was immaculate, but his back garden was overgrown. Eddie scanned through the darkness until he spotted the crummy birdhouse.

He sighed. "This is Mrs Nerdlinger's garden."

Rex cocked his head. "That's not possible."

"We counted the houses wrong. She's 47B, he's 47A. I can't see anything in this light. We need night vision gear or something."

Rex pulled a carrot from his coat pocket and passed it to Eddie. "My nan gave them to us, for seeing in the dark."

"A carrot?"

"Yeah, so we can see."

"We don't get instantaneous super-vision from one carrot. It's not like Popeye and spinach. Carrots are good for general eye health."

Rex's shadowy outline slumped. "So do you want a carrot or not?"

Eddie rolled his eyes. "Not now."

Rex's voice returned to a jovial tone. "I'll save it for later."

The pair crept to the fence that bordered Stork's back garden. As Eddie attempted to climb, Rex hauled him up by the legs, flipping him over the fence. Eddie thumped against the concrete pavement and groaned. Rex landed next to him, feet first with a spring to his knees. Placing his hands on the cold concrete, Eddie lifted himself until he felt a spasm in his lower back.

"Ouch!"

"You okay, Eddie?"

Eddie narrowed his eyes. "Shh, we need to be quiet, so we don't get caught."

"Cool, radio silence." Rex gave a thumbs up.

"Silence silence."

"Uh?"

"We have no radio. Just be quiet."

"Okay."

Rex and Eddie snuck up to Stork's bin. Rex lifted the lid, and Eddie untied the black bin bag. Inside they saw cans, tins, bottles, junk mail mixed in with food scraps, used microwave meal packets, tissues, and general household waste.

"He doesn't recycle," Eddie said.

"A-ha!" Rex said. "What does that mean?"

"It just means he doesn't recycle. Bit lazy."

"But no cat?"

"Doesn't look like it."

"How about now?" Rex grabbed the bin and tipped it over. The metal of the bin clanged against the concrete path.

"Shh!" Eddie said.

Rex tipped the bottom of the bin. The contents spewed out along the grass.

Eddie sighed. "Still no cat."

Rex scratched his head. "So he must be keeping Nubbin inside?"

Eddie approached the back door to Stork's home. He peered through the glass of the door. The house's open plan allowed a clear view of the kitchen and dining area through to the living room and front windows. Streetlight leaked in through the front blinds, giving the place an orange glow.

"It's pretty clean in there. Almost sterile."

Rex jolted his head into Eddie's view. "What was that? Did something move? A cat?" Rex jiggled the door handle. It was locked.

Eddie slapped Rex's hands away. "Stop it."

"We have the element of surprise." Rex pulled the

handle down harder. "We're coming to get you, Nubbin!"

The silhouette of Stork ran through the kitchen towards them. The pair ran towards the back of the garden as the inside lock turned and the back door burst open. Stork ran out in a dressing gown, swinging a cricket bat.

"What the hell do you think you're doing here?"

Rex and Eddie reached the back fence. Eddie reached for the top of the fence as Rex lifted him, but his lower back spasmed, and he dropped to the concrete. Stork came within batting distance as Eddie stood and raised his hands. Defeated, Rex followed suit.

"Sorry," Eddie said.

Rex nodded. "Yes, sorry. We thought we saw a cat."

"You idiots." Stork lowered the bat. "You can't go around like this. Scaring the crap out of people."

Rex stared at the lowered bat and grinned at Eddie. Eddie lightly shook his head so Stork wouldn't notice. Rex's eyes widened. Eddie shook his head again, a little more forcefully this time.

Eddie's back twinged, he lowered his hands to support himself. Stork stepped closer to him with the bat raised. Rex darted for the open kitchen door. Eddie took a step to the door, but Stork raised the bat.

Eddie stopped and raised his hands. "Fair enough."

Stork pointed the bat at Eddie. "You stay out here or I will knock you out."

With Eddie's back spasms, there was no way he'd outrun Stork. He nodded. "I accept your terms."

Stork rushed into the house while Rex darted around, calling out for Nubbin. He flung the bat towards Rex. Rex backed away and tripped over a low, modern sofa. The flying bat missed Rex's head and shattered a glass coffee table.

"You'll pay for that!" Stork shouted.

Rex shook his head, and shattered glass flew off his face. As he rolled onto his feet, Rex spat out a few more bits of glass. He wiped them away and found a spot of blood on his fingers.

He licked the blood. "You got me."

"I missed you. You broke my coffee table."

Rex's face scrunched up. "You broke your coffee table."

Stork grabbed Rex by the collar. Rex took a small shard of glass and used it to scratch Stork's arm.

"Ouch!" Stork's grip loosened.

Rex ran into the bedroom. "Kitty, Nubbin, Cleopatra?"

Stork chased after him.

At the back door, Eddie leaned his head into the kitchen. "Guys?" He spotted the bat on the floor, nodded, and entered. "Guys?"

"Get off the bed," Stork shouted, his voice muffled by the bedroom walls.

Eddie calmly studied the house. Everything was clean and tidy. Vertical blinds hung on every window. The furniture was made of leather, metal, and glass. A Roomba, the small automatic vacuum cleaner, rolled by.

"Rex!" he called out.

"Nubbin? Cleopatra?" Rex pounded out of the bedroom with Stork in pursuit.

Stork pointed at Eddie. "What did I tell you?"

"I know, stay at the fence, but—"

Stork stomped towards Eddie and stopped halfway. His eyes bulged as he held his chest. He gasped for air and dropped to his knees.

Rex stopped running and turned to Stork.

"He's having another heart attack," Eddie said.

"What do we do?"

The pair ran up to the man, unsure how to help. Both gave him an apologetic cringe. Stork rolled back, like he was about to fall down dead, but sprung forward with both his fists clenched. He punched Rex and Eddie's stomachs at the same time. Both detectives fell onto their backsides. Eddie clenched his teeth as his lower back throbbed at the same time as his stomach flexed and cramped.

Stork's face returned to its grey complexion as he stood.

"Faker." Rex coughed the words instead of saying them, his voice tight and shallow.

As Rex and Eddie searched for their breath, Stork towered over them.

"You're not decorators." He stepped over Eddie and picked up the bat. "Now, what's a Nubbin and who is Cleopatra?"

"Nubbin," Rex said with strain. "Cleopatra." He inhaled a short supply of air. "Cat."

"Two decorators broke into my house looking for a cat? Why?"

"Detectives," Rex said. "Mrs Nerd ... linger ... client."

"You think I stole her cat?"

Eddie shook his head.

Rex's top lip curled. "But ... I saw ... cat."

Eddie winced "He's ... allergic."

"He's a faker," Rex said, almost able to form a whole sentence now.

Eddie rolled to his side and lifted himself up. "No rugs, no felt couches, or curtains." He stood up. "This house is the most anti-allergen home I've seen."

Stork calmed a little. "Thank you."

Rex climbed up using the back of the sofa as support. "I saw a cat."

Eddie pointed at the Roomba whizzing around the

doorway. Rex sighed as his shoulders slumped.

"He can't be near a cat, let alone kidnap one."

Eddie hugged his hurting stomach and tried to massage his lower back with his outstretched hands. Stork sneered at Eddie's amateur contortion and turned to Rex, who shrugged his shoulders.

Eddie gave up trying to soothe himself and stood up straight. "Sorry for the disturbance."

Rex placed his hands on his hips. "Then why wouldn't he let us go through his bins?"

"Because it's weird," Stork said.

Eddie took a breath and nodded. "Yeah, I guess."

Stork folded his arms. "What about my coffee table?"

"What about it?"

Stork pointed at Rex. "You broke it."

Rex's jaw dropped. "You broke it throwing the bat at my head!"

Stork wagged his finger. "You moved, so it's your fault."

"So I've got to buy you a coffee table because I didn't block the bat with my head?"

"I'm not letting you leave until I'm compensated." Stork raised the cricket bat as he blocked the front door.

Rex stared at the back door and grinned at Eddie. Eddie gently shook his head so Stork wouldn't notice. Rex's eyes widened. Eddie shook his head again, a little more forcefully this time. Rex raised his eyebrows. Eddie sighed and nodded. The pair pushed past Stork and sprinted for the back door.

Stork followed, waving his bat. Rex shoved Eddie over the side fence into Mrs Nerdlinger's garden. As Rex lifted himself up the fence, Stork threw the bat. Rex's leg zipped over the top and missed the flying bat. It bounced off the fence and broke a small wind turbine on Stork's shed roof.

"You'll pay for that!" he shouted across the fence.

SIX

Rex and Eddie ran through Mrs Nerdlinger's back garden to her side gate. Eddie yanked the fence door open, but a tall man with a bushy beard blocked their way. Back-lit from the street lights, the man's figure seemed even more intimidating and bulky.

Eddie immediately assumed they were about to be strangled. Would he outlive Rex or die first? As a general shallow breather, he imagined he'd survive a throttling a bit longer than the average person. Eddie's mind raced through the possibilities, thinking hard, or at the very least worrying fast.

Rex didn't do any extra thinking. His fist swung forward and hit the bearded man in the face. The man punched Rex in the jaw, and he fell to the floor.

The man reached his fist back a second time. Eddie knew what was coming.

"But I didn't do anyth—"

Whack!

Eddie fell back. At least the pain of his swelling face distracted from his hurt stomach and back spasms.

The bearded man ran off into the street as Rex and Eddie rolled about on the floor.

"You hit him!" Eddie said.

"I know," Rex said, as shocked as Eddie. "I hit him square in the beard."

Eddie sat up and felt his nose. "My face hurts."

Rex crawled to the wall and helped himself up. "My face and hand hurt. It's like I whacked my hand against a brick covered in a Brillo-pad. It helped with the impact, but left me slightly itchy."

The pair stumbled into Mrs Nerdlinger's front garden as the man got into a white van across the street.

"We should follow, right?" Eddie asked. "So we can find Nubbin?"

Rex raised his eyebrows. "Can we?"

"I guess so. We've been chased before, but I've never been the chaser."

As the pair ran to the Morris Minor, the rusty van's engine rattled to life, and the man drove away.

Eddie sat in the driver's seat and turned the key. "Buckle up. As long as his van can't do more than sixty, we should keep pace."

Rex sneered as he fastened his seatbelt. "Don't make my first car chase a naff one, Eddie."

"This is an old car, I'm being practical."

The van drove down the street.

Rex tapped the dashboard. "This is no time to be practical. Floor it!"

Eddie checked his blind spot and turned into the street. "Here we go." He shoved his foot down hard on the accelerator, and the car's speedometer crept through the twenties.

The van turned right onto a major street.

"Faster, Eddie."

"I'm doing thirty-three in a residential area," Eddie protested.

The Morris Minor reached the end of the street and Eddie put his foot over the brake.

Rex raised his palms. "No braking."

"I have to yield to oncoming traffic."

"Then there'll be more cars between us and the van."

"They have the right of way," Eddie said.

As they approached the street corner, Eddie leaned forward to check for oncoming traffic. A silver Ford Focus raced up the street towards them. He stalled.

"Do it, Eddie! Don't let the Focus block our chase."

Eddie squeezed his eyes shut as he turned into the road with a screech of the tyres. He opened his eyes and found himself drifting into the opposing lane. He pulled right before they hit the other car. The white van was way ahead but in their sights.

Eddie took a deep breath. "We're gaining on him."

"Kind of." Rex gave a polite smile.

A loud, irate series of honks came from behind. The silver Ford Focus tailgated the Morris Minor as the driver honked.

Eddie checked the rear-mirror. "It's the car we cut off."

The driver shook his fist in between horn bashing. The Morris Minor's speed levelled off.

"You can do this, Eddie."

"I wasn't expecting a slight incline, we might lose him."

"That van's almost as crap as our car, he's slowed down too. Floor it."

Eddie pushed his foot down as far as it could go and the speedometer entered the forties. The Ford Focus wiggled side-to-side as it hovered almost bumper-to-bumper with the Morris Minor.

Exasperated, Eddie shouted to the rearview mirror: "I'm going over the speed limit, what more do you want?"

The van turned right into a smaller road.

"He's gone down Artemis Road," Eddie said. "That's downhill for a bit, we should catch up then."

Rex reclined in his seat. "Lovely stuff."

The Focus attempted to overtake by passing into the other lane. Annoyed, Eddie pulled to the left to close the gap. The Focus was headed straight for a pedestrian crossing island and braked. The driver pulled the Focus back in behind the Morris Minor.

"You could've let him go. We're turning right in a second."

Eddie squared up the rearview mirror and gave the driver an appropriate level of evil eye. "It's the principle of the thing. We're going over the speed limit, he shouldn't be so pushy."

The Focus let out a long beep.

Eddie flicked the right indicator as Artemis Road approached. He reached his right hand to the back window, gave the middle finger, and turned the Morris Minor onto the side road. The Focus whizzed past the junction while the driver watched the Morris Minor escape.

"Ha!" Eddie nodded.

The white van was back in their sights. The Morris Minor's speedometer crept past the mid-forties, well on its way to the fifties. Eddie changed into fifth gear and smiled at Rex. Rex bobbed his head, not impressed but having an okay time.

The Morris Minor reached a hundred yards behind the white van.

"If he turns left at the end of this street, then it's uphill. But right and we catch him."

Although adrenaline-fuelled, Eddie still checked his mirrors for safety. The lights of the car behind flicked on its high beams. The flashes caused Eddie to squint, unable to get a good view.

"We've got another weirdo behind us."

Rex turned back. "It's another silver Focus. Doesn't say much for the Focus customer base, does it?"

Eddie swallowed. "What?"

"I said, it doesn't say much for the Focus customer base."

In the mirror, Eddie saw the same erratic-waving hand. "It's the same man. He's followed us?"

Rex reached around to get a good view of the rear. The Focus headed straight for them "He's gaining on us."

Eddie gripped the steering wheel. "I thought we were the ones doing the pursuing. How'd we end up being chased?"

Rex tilted his head. "You gave him the finger."

"That's not a proper reason."

"You wouldn't let him pass."

Eddie squeezed the steering wheel. "That's not a good enough reason, either."

"And you cut him off."

"Because you told me to! This is your fault."

Rex raised his shoulders. "I'm just a passenger."

The white van reached the end of the road and turned right.

Eddie's eyes darted between the road ahead and the rearview mirror. He indicated a right turn.

"What are you telling him for?" Rex said.

"You're right." Eddie turned the steering wheel and rocked his head in frustration. The Focus followed, turning into the street with speed and grace.

The Morris Minor sped along at fifty-eight miles an hour.

Eddie grinned. "We're getting there, we're gonna catch him."

Rex tipped his head toward the rear. "What if the Focus catches us first?"

"I don't know."

"Will you fight him?"

Eddie's breathing became shallow. "Shut up, Rex. I'm concentrating."

"You might have to fight him."

"Please, Rex. Stop talking."

"It's okay, I hit the van driver," Rex said. "He was bigger than us and everything."

"I don't hit people."

"Me neither. I smile and try to look too innocent to be hit. Hitting him was, a bit risky."

"No, Rex. Not the parasite talk again. It was too dark to see, so I think maybe your survival instinct must've kicked in. Fight or flight."

"What?"

"It's instinct. In trouble, we have two choices: we fight or flight."

"Flight?"

"As in run away, or drive away in this case."

"You didn't run?"

"Because he blocked the exit."

"So were you gonna hit him, too?"

Eddie's chest pounded as the Focus's bumper tapped the back of the Morris Minor.

"I think I'm more flight or flight."

Rex nodded. "I see that."

The van approached a three-way junction at the end of the street.

"This is bad." Eddie winced. "That road opens up into a dual carriageway. The Focus can get up next to us and drive us into the trees."

"Or get in front," Rex said. "Then he could stop us, get out, and kill us."

Eddie narrowed his eyes at Rex. "Thanks for that."

The white van turned right into the road.

Eddie bit his bottom lip. The Focus bashed into them, which caused Eddie to bite down and whimper. He took a deep breath and indicated a left turn.

"You're indicating again?" Rex threw his hands in the air.

"Not quite."

Once the Morris Minor drove into the crossroad, Eddie pulled the steering wheel right and turned onto the street. The Focus, anticipating a left turn, carried along on its trajectory. It switched to the right to course correct but spun out of control. The Focus bumped over the concrete kerb and whacked against a line of thin trees.

"Woooooah," Eddie screamed.

Rex sat up straight, his jaw wide open. "That was amazing."

They got closer to the white van and Eddie slowed the car down to the fifty miles-per-hour speed limit.

Rex huffed. "What are you doing?"

"We can't maintain this speed."

"But things just got cool."

"In about a mile we start going uphill again. We'll lose him."

"So you're giving up?"

"He went off in a hurry trying to lose us. Since we've been so far behind, he's slowed down a bit. The man thinks he's lost us. If we stay back, he'll lead us to his home. Then we'll get to know who he is."

The Morris Minor tailed the white van, allowing a couple of cars between them and followed him down to a country lane under the motorway bridge, which crossed the Midway River.

The road under the bridge was poorly lit, further ahead it became an unlit country lane. Once the van travelled through the underpass, it disappeared into the darkness. The Morris Minor drove through the underpass. On the other side, nothing but the moon and stars lit the country lane. Eddie braked and watched for movement.

Rex leaned on the dashboard. "This is no time to stop."

Eddie tapped the steering wheel. "He's gone."

He reversed the Morris Minor towards the bridge until they passed a thin, muddy track that trailed the bridge towards the river.

Rex cranked the car window down and checked out the track. "Fresh tyre marks?"

Eddie turned into the lane and followed it. Once the river was in sight, Eddie pushed the brake. He turned off the car lights and engine.

"We have to sneak down there on foot, so we don't alert him."

Rex nodded. "Surprise him back. That'll show him."

The pair walked down the wet and muddy path, slipping and sliding along the way. They passed farmland and a pen of Shetland ponies. Rex reached out to stroke them, but Eddie pulled him along the bog-like path. Each step suctioned in the wet mud, by the time they reached the river they were both panting with exhaustion.

They crept up to the underpass by the river. Town lights from the other side of the river reflected hundreds of orange dots along the water and filled the riverbank with an amber hue. The moonlight highlighted the bridge's massive concrete pillars. The shadows of the pillars fell on each side of the white van, now parked by a small caravan at the river's edge.

Eddie pulled out a pair of binoculars to get a look at the caravan's windows. The blinds were closed. The sound of hundreds of cars speeding along the motorway above them allowed them to talk at a reasonable level without alerting their attacker.

"Can I use the binoculars?" Rex asked.

"Next time."

The owner of the van exited the caravan. He was dressed in a black trench coat, a wool hat, and muddy, grey mountain boots. He approached a pillar, unzipped his fly, and peed against the concrete.

Rex leaned towards Eddie. "Is this a crime?"

"Peeing against the wall? I think so."

"No, us watching him pee?"

"No, well…" Eddie bobbed his head left and right. "Maybe. He started it by peeing."

"But we're consenting?"

"No, we're not."

"We did walk down here."

"Not to see him pee," Eddie snapped.

Alerted by Eddie's raised voice, the man's head darted in their direction. The whites of his eyes bulged. He zipped up and ran to his van.

"The man has excellent control," Rex said. "I couldn't stop peeing like that."

The pair attempted to run, but the clumps of mud around their feet had an anchor-like effect. As Rex wobbled, he grabbed Eddie for support, accidentally pulling Eddie down with him.

Eddie put his hands out for stability, but his palms glided through the puddle's surface.

"Rex, you—" Eddie's face went splat into a puddle.

The bearded man ran to his van and drove off down a path that followed the river.

Rex pulled Eddie up as best as he could. Eddie coughed up brown water as he got back on his feet.

"You okay, Eddie?"

Eddie stared at Rex.

"You don't need mouth-to-mouth, do you?"

"I most certainly do not."

"We should run back to the car, right?"

Eddie pulled his suctioned foot from the mud. "I'm not gonna try running again."

The pair surveyed the scene, using their phone screens as dim lights. Amongst a little camping area, they found a stove and a weathered camping chair. The caravan's tyres were flat. It seemed the man had lived under the bridge for some time.

Eddie opened the caravan door. A waft of a musty odour attacked their nostrils. Inside the caravan was tidy, but the flooring had warped. The top cupboards contained tinned food, and the bed was neatly made. Rex and Eddie rummaged around.

"No personal effects," Eddie said. "Nothing to identify him."

They trudged towards the car, stopping for Rex to feed a Shetland pony his spare carrot. As the pony bit off a chunk and chewed, a cat walked along the fence and sniffed the carrot in Rex's hand.

"Eddie," Rex whispered, so as not to disturb the feline. "Do you recognise that cat?"

He looked at the fluffy, grey tabby. "Professor Buttons?"

"It is. That man kidnapped Professor Buttons. He must be some obsessed stalker or something."

Eddie raised his eyebrows. "You think he's spent years tormenting Mrs Nerdlinger and her cats?"

"What a horrible git."

Rex called out to the cat as he approached. He slowly reached out his hands. The cat jumped onto his shoulders.

Eddie shrugged. "That works."

Rex grinned as he rubbed under the cat's chin.

"Come on." Eddie waved Rex towards the car. "Let's get the cat back to Mrs Nerdlinger and find a way to identify this weirdo."

SEVEN

In the morning, Rex and Eddie returned to Mrs Nerdlinger's house with the fluffy grey tabby. As they walked across the garden, Professor Buttons happily lounged in Rex's arms. They knocked on the door, but there was no answer.

Rex scratched his head. "Do we leave the cat here?"

Eddie huffed. "Seems like a bit of an anticlimax." He tried to peek through the door's frosty window panel. "We should get a thank you, or a hug, or something."

Rex nodded. "A hug would be a nice tip. We could hug each other instead?"

A loud groan bellowed from next door. "Will you stop your incessant yapping?" Ian Stork shouted from his front window.

The pair flinched, expecting Stork to chase after them. He stayed at his computer, peering over his monitor. "Some of us are trying to work."

"We're working as well," Eddie said. "We're waiting for Mrs Nerdlinger."

Stork stood. "What day is it?"

Eddie thought about it. "Tuesday."

"What time is it?"

He checked his watch. "Nine-forty."

"Now, where would a teacher be at this time of day?"

"School?" Rex asked.

Stork threw his hands in the air. "What amazing powers of deduction!"

"Thanks for your help," Rex said, unaware of Stork's aggression. He scooted down the path until Eddie grabbed his arm.

"It's a trick. Why would he help us?"

"I'm not helping you." Stork stepped to the open window. "I'm getting rid of you. I need to concentrate on my stocks."

Eddie gave an agreeable shrug, and the duo marched down the patio.

Stork stuck his head out the window to call out. "That said, I am invested in your case. Once she pays you, I want my money for the coffee table."

Eddie marched along the pavement. Rex followed with Professor Buttons resting across his shoulders. The pair approached St Jude Primary School, a one-story building on top of a small, grassy bank. The front of the building was a line of small classrooms facing the street. The classes had white, plastic boarding with tiny windows across the centre. Red brick pillars separated each room. Banners covered the chain link fence on the street, advertising upcoming events and inviting parents to collect supermarket vouchers for the school's fundraiser.

Rex and Eddie stood on the pavement, examining their old school.

"It looks the same," Eddie said.

Rex cocked his head. "Only smaller."

Inside, a pink laminated floor covered in scuff marks reflected the fluorescent lighting from above. The bottom half of the walls were painted yellow while the top half had been decorated with children's artwork. Displays included local Cloisterham landmarks, mosaics of animals, and an off-putting civil war battle made of cut out cavaliers and roundheads. Close to the entrance, a glass window gave a view of the receptionist's office. A plump, grey-haired receptionist typed at her desk.

"May I help you?"

Eddie nodded. "We're here to see Mrs Nerdlinger."

She pulled a timeworn intercom microphone attached to a wooden stand and pushed the red button. Her voice echoed throughout the hallway.

"Mrs Nerdlinger to reception, Mrs Nerdlinger to reception." She pushed the microphone away. "You can wait in the library area."

The pair turned to an alcove of full bookshelves. Eddie searched for a place to sit but only saw plastic, child-size chairs dotted along the blue nylon carpet.

In the corner, a ten-year-old boy faced the wall. He wore the school uniform which was a white shirt, red tie, a blue v-neck jumper, grey trousers, and black shoes. The boy turned and stared at Professor Buttons.

"Face the wall!" the receptionist said.

"What did he do?" Rex asked.

"None of your business." She gave a forceful nod and returned to typing.

Eddie studied the noticeboard announcements for fetes, a parents evening, and fundraisers. Rex pulled up a tiny chair and checked out the books.

Mrs Nerdlinger's arrival was announced by her sandals

smacking against the linoleum flooring. She wore black trousers and a long-sleeved pink top with a high neckline. Her auburn hair was up in a knot. Despite her down-to-earth attire, there was still a magnetism to her that made the pair blush when they saw her.

"Rex and Eddie? So good to see you." Mrs Nerdlinger petted the cat on Rex's shoulders. "And who is this cutie?"

"Professor Buttons," Rex said.

The boy wrinkled his nose. "The cat's a professor?"

"Face the wall," Eddie said.

Mrs Nerdlinger held out her hand for the cat to smell. "It can't be."

"It is." Eddie lowered his voice so the boy couldn't hear. "We found a man trying to break into your house. We followed him to his hideout under the motorway bridge. That's where we found your cat."

"What side of the bridge?" the boy asked.

Mrs Nerdlinger placed her hands on her hips. "Jeremy Platt, you will speak only when spoken to or I shall add another week of detention."

The boy faced the wall. "Sorry, Miss."

Mrs Nerdlinger leaned in to whisper. "A stalker stole Professor Buttons?"

Eddie nodded. "He's a homeless man."

"A caravan can be a home," Rex said.

"What do I call him then?"

Rex shrugged. "House-less?"

"No, I don't like that," Eddie said. "I live in a flat. I'm house-less. I don't want to be in the same category as him."

The cat climbed into Mrs Nerdlinger's arms.

"Did you catch him?" she asked.

Eddie shook his head. "He got away, but left behind your cat."

She stroked the feline as he climbed onto her shoulders. "Professor Buttons is alive?"

"We think the stalker followed you for years, so he probably took Buttons—"

"*Professor* Buttons," Mrs Nerdlinger said.

"Yes, sorry. Professor Buttons, and kept him all this time."

Rex nodded. "I bet he has Nubbin, too."

"He does?" She turned to Eddie. "You're going to get Nubbin too?"

Rex sat back down on the tiny chair and picked up a book. "Of course we are."

Eddie grimaced. "Well, I mean maybe it's a police matter. He'll likely be armed after we scared him."

"Oh please? I tried the police before you. They aren't interested. I need you to do it."

Eddie pursed his lips but softened after looking into her blue-grey eyes for a tad too long.

"We can't do it for nothing," he said. "We already solved one case, pro-bono."

"No, you didn't. The case was Nubbin, and you haven't found Nubbin. Now that you know where he is, you're trying to extort me for money?"

"It's not like that."

"I'm a teacher, do you know how much we get paid?"

"More than nothing," Eddie muttered.

"Can you speak louder, so the rest of us can hear?"

"Nothing," Eddie said with attitude.

Rex lunged up from the little plastic chair, nature book in hand. "Froglet!"

Eddie, Mrs Nerdlinger, Jeremy Platt, and the receptionist all turned to Rex.

He smiled. "A baby frog is a froglet." He tapped the book. "Miss, I found the answer."

Mrs Nerdlinger nodded. "Very good, Rex."

"It says here a tadpole is actually when it has legs and a tail. When it's just got a tail, it's called a polliwog. Why don't we call them that? It's much more fun. I think polliwog's my word of the day."

She smiled at Eddie. "Please do tell me you will go and rescue Nubbin from this man?"

Eddie thought he would successfully resist her charms this time, especially with her modest work clothes, but with her hair up, he noticed her perfectly even ears.

He slouched. "Fine, we'll check his hideout tonight."

Rex and Eddie strolled out of the school reception towards the street.

"Excuse me," a loud voice said. The pair turned around to see a tall man in his fifties with a thick, grey beard wag his finger. "Stop right there."

They paused as the man approached. He wore a dark-green trench coat with a woolly scarf dangling around his neck. "Are you the owner of the Morris Minor?"

"Who's asking?" Eddie's heart pounded as the bearded man marched closer.

He had the height, the beard, he recognised their car.

Is this the cat thief? Eddie thought.

"I'm Mr Jeffries, the head teacher."

"We, uh, walked here," Eddie said.

The tall man scuttled down the small grassy bank and caught up with them. "You're Mrs Nerdlinger's detectives?"

Rex leaned in and stared at the man's chin. He clenched a fist and studied his hand as he compared the beard to the one he punched last night.

Mr Jeffries shuffled back, uneasy.

Eddie held out his hand. "What can we help you with?"

The teacher shook Eddie's hand but still gave Rex a jittery look.

"I'm trying to find the owners of that car." He pointed to their Morris Minor.

Rex grinned. "Oh, that's easy—"

"Why?" Eddie interrupted.

"They ran me off the road last night and damaged my Ford Focus. Never thought I'd see them again, but here they are outside the school. What luck!"

Eddie feigned a smile. "What luck, indeed."

"You are Mrs Nerdlinger's detective's aren't you?"

Rex gave a proud nod while Eddie hesitantly followed.

"Do you have the ability to trace a car to an owner. What's the procedure?"

"You want to hire us?" Rex asked, excited.

"I was hoping to get a few pointers. I don't think I could afford to hire an actual detective on a teacher's wage."

"You could afford us," Rex said. "We're dead cheap."

Eddie kicked Rex's shin. "He means we're competitively priced and efficient."

"We are?"

Eddie kicked Rex's shin again, harder this time. "I bet we could find your person so quickly, we'd hardly have any hours to bill you at all."

"You're that good?"

Rex drew in his breath. Eddie pursed his lips at Rex.

Eddie looked over the hedge at the Morris Minor, pretending to examine the car. "You're sure that's the same car?"

"I memorised the registration plate."

"Have you considered...," Eddie's mind was blank. "Not finding them?"

"You don't understand, my Ford Focus is only three-years-old, and they ruined it. I planned to drive that car into my retirement. I can't pay for expensive bodywork."

Eddie pointed at the beat-up Morris Minor. "You think they can afford body work? Suing them would be a waste of time."

"So you're saying, I'll have to wait for them to come to the car and confront them man-to-man."

Eddie bit his bottom lip. "It looks abandoned? Right, Rex?"

"Oh yeah, it's so sad and old."

Mr Jeffries put his hands on his hips. "They drove it last night."

Eddie repeatedly nodded, waiting for inspiration.

Rex scratched his chin. "Maybe it was a joyride!"

"Yes." Eddie nodded. "A joyride."

Rex smiled with his whole face. "I bet some teens drove it all night and dumped it here."

Eddie nodded. "Good story— Uh, theory. The owner is probably some sweet, retired old lady."

"They didn't drive like joyriders." Mr Jeffries said. "They drove slow."

"Are you sure?" Eddie folded his arms. "Are you sure they weren't going the speed limit? Maybe even a little over?"

Mr Jeffries nodded sharply. "I'm sure. It wasn't a joyrider. It had to be the owner."

"My professional recommendation is to leave it. I'm positive the owner of that car won't come near it."

Eddie gave a departing nod. He and Rex walked down the path.

Mr Jeffries sighed. "You're right. I should smash up

their car as much as they smashed up mine and call it even."

Eddie stopped and turned. "Or you could forgive them. Maybe give them the benefit of the doubt?"

"No, you were right earlier. They can't afford body-work, so I should smash up their car in return."

"I don't think that's exactly what I said."

Mr Jeffries marched towards the street. "Thanks for all your advice."

He grabbed a shovel next to a gardener working on the school grounds. He nodded at Rex and Eddie, ran at the Morris Minor waving the shovel, and bashed in the passenger door several times.

Rex and Eddie dawdled down the path.

"What do we do now?" Rex whispered. "Do we stop him?"

Eddie checked out the damaged Ford Focus in the staff car park. The passenger side was roughened by the impact, with the lights and mirror smashed. "It's not too much damage. I guess we wait until he's done."

They slowed down more as they approached the street.

Mr Jeffries took off his coat and scarf. "This is quite the workout." He flung the coat and scarf on a hedge. "Do you want to help?"

Eddie waved his hands. "No, thank you."

Rex bobbed his head, thinking it over.

"No, Rex," Eddie whispered.

"He's gonna do it in anyway. I've never got to smash up a car."

"You're not doing it."

"The sooner he finishes, the sooner we can go."

Eddie sighed. "Fine, but no more damage than the Focus."

"Coming." Rex ran to the car with a dainty skip and kicked in the bonnet's side.

Mr Jeffries passed him the shovel. "Give this a go!"

Rex grabbed the shovel "Can I do the side mirror?"

"Be my guest."

He decapitated the mirror in one swoop.

Eddie sat on the brick wall and watched them whack in the Morris Minor. He'd never seen Rex so happy.

EIGHT

The Morris Minor drove through the motorway bridge's underpass and turned onto the trail that ran alongside it. Eddie parked the car before they reached the riverbank.

After shutting off the engine, he pulled the handbrake. "We need to sneak up to his campsite on foot to avoid scaring him off again."

Rex leaned towards Eddie.

Eddie pulled back. "What are you doing?"

"My door doesn't open now, so I've got to get out your side."

Eddie rolled his eyes. "Perfect. Come on."

The pair exited from Eddie's side and trudged through the mud. Eddie looked back to check out Rex's side of the car. The body had the texture of a crumpled piece of paper. It didn't seem as bad in the dark, which made Eddie feel marginally better.

Rex and Eddie stepped through the muddy path to the nearest pillar. Although the white van wasn't there now, they kept their distance as they watched the caravan for movement. They spied as the sun went down.

"I need the bathroom," Rex said.

"You'll have to go outside."

Rex pouted as he approached the bridge wall. He unzipped and peed against the concrete. Rex leaned against the corner to search the area.

"Who's that?" Rex whispered. "Upon the mound."

Eddie pointed the binoculars at the raised concrete mound supporting the bridge. In the dark corner stood a figure.

"We're being watched."

"Is that him?" Rex asked, mid-stream.

"Will you stop that!"

"I told you, I can't stop once I've started."

"You're jeopardising the case!" Eddie barked.

"Don't shout. I can't go when I'm nervous."

"Good," Eddie snapped.

"Fine, you win." Rex zipped up, "I can't pee anymore."

Eddie lowered the binoculars. "I think he's on a bicycle. If we make any sudden movements, he might ride off. It's too risky. I say we wave the white flag and talk to him."

"You brought a white flag?"

"Not literally, it's an expression."

Rex and Eddie stepped out into the open with their hands raised.

"Hey," Eddie called out. "We want to talk."

Rex shook his fist.

"What are you doing? You look aggressive."

"I'm waving a white flag."

"No, you aren't."

"Not literally."

"Stop it."

"Sorry," Rex called out to the man. "I meant to wave a white flag, but we don't have one."

The man got on the bicycle seat.

"Please don't go," Eddie said.

The bike sped down the mound towards them.

Rex stepped to the side. "Is he gonna ram us?"

As the cyclist got close, he braked, stopping shy of Eddie's toes. The moonlight revealed the cyclist's face, Jeremy Platt.

"Why are you here?" Eddie said.

"I'm looking for Mrs Nerdlinger's cat."

"You've no business looking for her cat."

"I've got two weeks of detention left. That means I've got to face the wall every break for two weeks straight. I'm in her bad books."

Eddie rolled his eyes. "You're being paranoid."

"No seriously, she has a little black book which she writes in when people are bad. If I find the cat she'll be so happy she'll forgive me, and I'll be in her good books."

"She has a good book, too?" Rex asked.

Jeremy scoffed. "No, don't be ridiculous."

"Go home." Eddie shooed at him. "This is dangerous work."

The boy tutted. "You managed to do it with Doctor Bubbles."

Eddie folded his arms. "Professor Buttons."

"Whatever."

"If you want to be in her good books, you'll want to get the cat's name right."

Rex nodded. "She is particular."

Eddie put his hands on his hips. "Isn't staring at a wall for two weeks easier than finding a cat from a deranged homeless man? Why not wait it out?"

"Because, the other boys are making moves on my girl."

Eddie sneered. "Your girl?"

"Tracy, she's the most beautiful girl in the playground. Now that I've got detention, the other boys are working their angles, chatting her up and stuff. She's gonna forget about me."

"In two weeks?"

"She has needs. I got to be around her, or she'll move on. Don't you have to impress your girlfriend?"

Rex and Eddie grumbled.

"We haven't got girlfriends." Rex perked up. "But Eddie got dumped recently." He nodded to Eddie as if to say, 'Well done.'

"What happened?" Jeremy asked.

"She, uh, moved on."

Jeremy shook his head. "A relationship is like an orchid, it needs a lot of care and attention to flower."

"That's good," Rex said. "I feel like I should write that down." He eyed Eddie's notepad.

Eddie shook his head. "This is for official detective business."

"He's part of the investigation now. We can at least make it a footnote or something."

Eddie sneered. "How can you take relationship advice from a boy with his first girlfriend?"

Jeremy tilted his head. "Fifth."

"Fifth?" Eddie said, loud enough for an echo.

"Yeah, why? How many you had?"

"Like three. Well, maybe two and a half."

Rex raised his index finger. "Just the one."

"How old are you two?"

"Twenty-eight," Rex said.

69

He looked them both up and down. "How many boyfriends have you had?"

"None," Eddie said.

"You two aren't … together?"

Eddie narrowed his eyes. "We're business partners."

Rex grabbed Eddie's shoulder, and pointed to a pillar close to the water where a cat sat in the shadows. Its yellow eyes shined out at them.

Jeremy raced his bike towards the cat. Rex and Eddie ran after him, but couldn't keep up with a twenty-one gear bike. The cat backed up into a corner, walled in by a chain fence.

"Stop!" Eddie shouted. "You'll scare it."

Jeremy gently got off his bike. "Here, kitty kitty."

Eddie tiptoed towards the cat. "Nubbin."

Rex followed. "Meow."

Eddie bared his teeth. "What was that?"

"I'm trying to speak his language."

Jeremy placed his duffel bag on the ground and quietly unzipped it. He pulled out a colourful feather on a rod.

Eddie scoffed at Rex. "You can speak cat, I assume?"

"I just said meow."

As they argued, Jeremy waved the feather to get the cat's attention. It bounded towards the feather.

Eddie shook his head. "Why'd you think he'd react to meow? It could mean anything from 'dinner's ready' to 'Heil Hitler.'"

Rex screwed up his face. "You think it's a Nazi cat?"

The cat followed Jeremy's feather. Jeremy pulled the rod, flinging it into the bag. The cat jumped and landed inside. He zipped up the bag, gaining the detectives' attention. Tossed the bag over his shoulder, Jeremy cycled past them. Rex and Eddie ran to the Morris Minor.

Eddie unlocked the door. "We need to get that cat before he gets to Mrs Nerdlinger's."

He climbed into his seat and buckled up while Rex waited outside.

Eddie threw up his hands. "What are you doing?"

"My side is broken."

Eddie unbuckled and climbed out. Rex leapt through the driver's door into his seat.

Eddie got back in. "Seatbelts."

They buckled in unison. Eddie reversed the Morris Minor out of the muddy track. Once they hit the real road, he spun the car into the direction of Jeremy, who cycled with gusto. The Morris Minor reached thirty miles per hour as they passed Jeremy.

Eddie smiled. "We have the advantage, there's two of us."

The Morris Minor parked in the middle of the street. As Eddie got out, he slammed his door, not realising Rex was trying to get out from Eddie's side.

"Let's get him, Rex."

Jeremy swerved past as Eddie spun around trying to grab him.

Eddie searched for his partner. "Rex?"

The car door opened wide enough to tap Eddie on the back. He turned around and saw Rex inside on all fours.

"Sorry, Eddie. My door again."

Eddie shoved Rex back into his seat. He sat down, buckled up, and started the car.

The Morris Minor gained on Jeremy, but Eddie gingerly braked when the traffic lights turned red. Jeremy glided by on his bike in the brief second before the cars opposite moved forward.

Eddie grumbled. "Perfect."

"Just go."

"I can't, this isn't a bike. We're beholden to the rules of the road."

"Oh, I get it," Rex said. "You're sabotaging the case to prove how reasonable you are."

"I most certainly am not!"

"You don't want to take risks because it means you have the cat parasite."

"I'm following the rules, so we don't get chased by an angry driver again."

Rex folded his arms. "Whatever."

The traffic light turned green. Eddie floored the accelerator so fast, the tyres screeched as they sped off. The Morris Minor caught up with the bike again. Eddie revved the engine.

"Easy, Eddie. You look like you're gonna run him over."

"I'm gonna wear him out for a bit, then we can snatch the cat from him."

"Nice," Rex said.

"He's stuck with us now."

Jeremy gave a cheeky smile as he rode onto the pavement. He swung left into an alleyway between a military graveyard and a school field.

Eddie slammed on the brake. "I can't follow him down there. We've got a massive detour." He thumped the steering wheel. "He's gonna get there before us."

"Maybe if we tell Mrs Nerdlinger he stole the cat, we'll still get the credit."

Eddie peered over Rex's shoulder out the passenger window. The entrance to the military graveyard was open. He thought about the two hundred pound reward Mrs Pickles offered for the cat.

"It's been a few years, but I think the graveyard runs alongside the alleyway?" Eddie said.

Rex's eyes lit up. "You want to drive through the graveyard?"

Eddie grimaced. "There's no street lighting, and I'm sure it's illegal to go over five miles an hour."

"Too risky?" Rex mocked.

Eddie took a deep breath. Jeremy's smug smile repeated in his mind. He pulled the steering wheel left. "That two hundred pounds will be ours yet."

The Morris Minor barrelled through the graveyard entrance. The bumpy road rattled the pair in their seats. As the car sped through the graveyard, a few teens drinking alcopops jumped from the various gravestones and hid behind a cannon statue on a concrete pedestal, the most robust obstacle available.

"Are you okay, Eddie?"

"I'm not letting that little brat steal our reward money."

Along the edge of the cemetery, a two-foot brick wall separated them from the alleyway. They were neck-and-neck with Jeremy until the graveyard's road turned right. The Morris Minor clipped over the curb onto the green, Eddie braked before they hit the end wall.

"But Mrs Nerdlinger isn't offering a reward," Rex said.

Jeremy rolled past, waving. Eddie bolted out of the car.

Rex rolled out of the driver's door onto the grass. "You were gonna give Nubbin to Mrs Pickles this whole time."

Eddie cautiously climbed over the two-foot wall. "I was gonna talk to you about it." He ran along the alleyway as Rex sprang over the wall.

Jeremy slowed as he hit a hill. He lowered his gears, which clicked and clacked in the struggle to change. Eddie gained on him. Eddie's guts throbbed as his heart raced, but he was determined to get the cat. Both Rex and Eddie could almost touch the bagged cat. At the top of the hill,

Eddie launched for the bag, knocking Rex into a fence in the process. His fingers felt the cloth of the bag's handle until a fallen Rex stretched out his foot and tripped Eddie. Eddie tumbled into the dirty alley while Jeremy glided downhill with speed. As Jeremy rode off into the distance, he gave the pair the finger.

"You're a liar." Rex crossed his arms and legs.

Eddie got back on his feet. "I'm not a liar, I never said Mrs Nerdlinger would get the cat."

"You said we'd do my idea of working out who the owner is once we got the cat."

"I know, and once we got the cat, I was gonna convince you we had to give the cat to Mrs Pickles."

"Why? Because she was the rightful owner or because she'll pay money?"

"Mrs Pickles did say she had the cat before the tail. Mrs Nerdlinger said the cat only visited at that point."

Eddie offered his hand to help Rex up.

Rex tightened his crossed arms. "That's why you were gonna give the cat to Mrs Pickles?"

Eddie gave a small rapid nod. Rex narrowed his eyes.

"Fine, it was because she paid more."

Rex jumped to his feet and wagged his finger. "I knew it."

"Because we're broke." Eddie sighed. "Before we took this case, we barely had enough money for a tank of petrol, and this case costs petrol. We've barely got enough money for two pints. You want to give the cat to Mrs Nerdlinger because you like her."

"She's nice, but I still wanted to work it out with you. I thought we were business partners." Rex leaned on a fence, defeated. "And I thought you liked my idea."

"We are business partners, but the business part only

works if we are a business. That means we need to make money."

"And the partner bit only works if we both have a say." Rex slid down the fence until he sat on the ground.

Eddie lowered to the tarmac to sit next to him. "I'm sorry, Rex. We are partners."

"Business partners." Rex grinned. "So, what do we do now?"

"Nothing, I guess. Mrs Nerdlinger's got Professor Buttons and Nubbin. We scared off the bearded man. We go home. Take the loss."

Rex's voice softened. "And you said we've got enough money for two pints?"

Eddie cracked a half smile. He pulled out the change in his pocket. "Just about."

The pair shuffled along the alley towards the cemetery. As Rex climbed over the wall, Eddie stared at a telephone post.

"What's that, Eddie?"

He didn't say anything. Rex climbed back over the wall and joined him. A missing cat poster was stapled to the telephone pole. It offered a reward of one hundred pounds for the return of a fluffy, grey tabby cat with a full mane.

"That wasn't Professor Buttons," Eddie said. "We stole someone else's cat."

NINE

Eddie pulled the Morris Minor up close to Mrs Nerdlinger's street as Jeremy knocked on her door.

"It's fine," Eddie said. "She's getting Nubbin back now, so she can't be angry at us. We'll just explain the situation and take Professor Buttons."

Rex held the poster they tore from the pole. "It might be a different cat."

"A grey tabby cat with black stripes that lives in the area we took him from."

"It might be a *black* tabby cat with *grey* stripes, you don't know."

From the car they watched Mrs Nerdlinger open the door to Jeremy.

"Let's go get Professor Buttons, I mean, what's his name?"

Rex checked the poster. "Dave."

"Right, let's go get Dave."

The pair exited the car and walked to the house. As they approached, Jeremy unzipped the bag in front of Mrs Nerdlinger, and the cat's head popped out.

"Oh, Nubbin." Mrs Nerdlinger said, her hands on her heart.

"This is perfect timing," Eddie whispered. "She'll be so happy she'll completely understand about Professor Buttons, I mean Dave."

She lifted the cat from the bag, revealing a tall, bushy tail. Mrs Nerdlinger's smile dropped. "This isn't Nubbin."

Rex and Eddie slumped. Mrs Nerdlinger's face turned as pale as porcelain. She seemed so delicate, she could shatter before their eyes.

Jeremy raised his chin. "Nubbin's missing a tail?"

"That's why her name is Nubbin." Mrs Nerdlinger pat Jeremy on the shoulder. "Be sure you put him back where you found him. I'm sure he'll make his own way home from there."

At any other time, Rex and Eddie would want to rub it in Jeremy's face, but not today. They watched the crowd of cats eat food from her patio. The fluffy, grey tabby chewed away amongst his new brothers and sisters.

She nodded at the pair. "At least I've still got Professor Buttons; home at last."

Jeremy stepped off the patio, disappointed. "See you in detention tomorrow, Miss."

"Let's take a break tomorrow," she said.

He smiled and rode his bike. When Mrs Nerdlinger wasn't looking, he gave Rex and Eddie the finger again.

"What can I do for you boys?"

Rex and Eddie's eyes wandered around the garden. Neither could look her in the face.

"We just wanted to make sure..." Eddie took a deep breath. "We're checking to see that Professor Buttons settled in okay."

Rex's face screwed up. "What?"

"Oh, he's doing fine," Mrs Nerdlinger said. "It's like he was never away."

"Good," Eddie nodded. "Good to hear that then. Well, we should be off."

"Really?" Rex said. "Haven't you got something else to say?"

"No, no." Eddie gave a theatrical yawn. "I'm ready to call it a night. Unless Rex, you've got something you'd like to say to Mrs Nerdlinger?"

Rex's head darted between Eddie and their client. She looked miserable. "No. Nothing to report."

"Are you sure, Rex? You seemed like you really wanted to tell her something?"

He shook his head.

"Fine, we'll be on our way. Goodbye, Miss."

"Goodbye, Eddie. Goodbye, Rex." She sat on the patio, her face ready to crack. It was evident that once they'd left, Mrs Nerdlinger was going to cry.

At the Morris Minor, Rex crawled over the driver's side to his seat. Eddie got in and shut the door.

"What was that?" Rex asked.

"We can't ask Mrs Nerdlinger to give up Professor Buttons, she's already upset about Nubbin."

"She's a mature lady. Mrs Nerdlinger will understand when you tell her," Rex said.

"I'm not telling her."

"Well, I can't do it."

The pair sat in silence.

"We just have to take the cat," Eddie said.

Rex's jaw dropped. "But——"

"Do you want to tell her?"

"No."

Eddie grasped the steering wheel. "Then we need to steal back Dave, and return him to his rightful owner."

Having parked around the corner, the pair crawled along the street towards Mrs Nerdlinger's home. The duo squatted alongside a hedge to get a look of the house.

"Can you see anything?"

Rex held the binoculars to his eyes and surveyed Ian Stork's home. "His lights are off?"

"What about Mrs Nerdlinger?"

He turned to the right and viewed her home. All of the lights were off. "It's clear."

Eddie reached for the binoculars. "Let me check."

"No, you said I could use them next time. It's my turn."

"I didn't think next time would be so important."

He reached again, but Rex slapped away his hands. A jogger passed by and stopped to cross the road. She jogged on the spot and checked for traffic until Rex and Eddie caught her eye.

Eddie panicked. I *need to look inconspicuous, or at least busy. Why would I be here? I'll examine the hedge, like a … like a hedge examiner? That's too stupid.*

He looked over to Rex, who pantomimed examining the hedge. Eddie copied him, pulled at the leaves and nodded like he approved. Rex and Eddie both smiled at the jogger. She crossed the street, running a little faster than before.

The pair snuck into the alley behind Mrs Nerdlinger's house and entered the back garden. With the interior lights off, there was little to illuminate the grass.

"Beware the poo," Eddie said.

"About the poo," Rex said. "I know you don't want to talk about it, but since we're breaking into our old teacher's house to steal a cat we already stole from a stranger, I was wondering…"

"Yes?"

"You know, the cat poo parasite lives in your brain and makes you take more risks."

"Please, Rex. I can't think about toxoplasma right now."

The pair crept across the grass towards the house.

"But our choices might be evidence for the parasite, right?"

"I really can't think about a parasite swimming about my brain. It makes my whole head itch."

"I texted my mate, Jim Jams, and he says fifty percent of people have the parasite, so it's pretty normal."

"You're not helping."

"He said there are far more likely and worse parasites in the average person's brain."

"Again, not helping. We don't have the parasite for one excellent reason; this isn't risky."

"Breaking into Mrs Nerdlinger's house isn't risky?"

"No, it's cowardly. We're doing it because we are far too scared of her reaction. So you see, we're cowards."

Rex narrowed his eyes and then nodded. He smiled. "Cool."

"Eddie, what about when you cut off the Focus driver? Or sped through a graveyard? Those weren't risky?"

"Not now, Rex."

They reached the back door, and Rex poked his hand through the cat flap. Cracks of street lighting through the drawn curtains revealed little. Eddie pulled at the doormat under Rex. "Move out the way, I'm gonna check for a key."

Rex climbed off, and Eddie pulled up the mat. No key. Eddie lifted various plant pots. The pair pulled the heaviest pot to one side, which revealed the key. Eddie unlocked the door. As he pulled, the door creaked open.

"Dave," Eddie whispered.

"Dave the cat," Rex called out.

"Oh, thanks for clarifying," Eddie said. "I'm sure the cat thought you meant some other Dave."

"It's a common name."

Rex poked his head inside, sniffed the air, and stepped in. He turned on the switch. The lights revealed over a hundred boxes from floor to ceiling, turning each room into a maze. Eddie climbed over and checked a couple of boxes. They contained empty cans, newspapers, old textbooks, magazines, encyclopedias, and a jar of inch-long used pencils.

Rex's forehead creased up. "How does she live like this?"

The pair gazed at the labyrinth of tripping hazards. At their feet was a bowl filled with cat food and a full litter tray.

"She doesn't," Eddie said. "She delivers the food and removes the faeces." Eddie covered his mouth with his sleeve. "I think she uses this house as storage and lives somewhere else."

Rex nodded. "Like the Little Mermaid's grotto."

Eddie frowned. "No, not like that."

"She's a pretty redhead who hoards things. I bet if Ariel hadn't found Prince Eric, she'd have gone on to become a catfish lady."

Eddie scoured the boxes, searching for the cat.

"Dave the cat?" Rex made kissing noises. "Dave the cat?"

The tabby cat tottered along and rubbed against Rex's leg.

"You can just call him Dave, he knows he's a cat."

They locked up the back door and returned the key.

As the pair walked back to the Morris Minor, they passed an old, blue Saab with faded paint and no hubcaps. Inside a woman slept surrounded by boxes filling the seats.

"Mrs Nerdlinger?" Rex said. "How does she manage to live like this?"

Eddie shrugged. "Launderettes, gyms, take-out food. I guess she gets by." He nodded at the cat. "Let's get him back to his rightful owner."

Rex stroked the tabby. "Sorry, you had to see that, Dave."

TEN

Rex and Eddie approached a barn converted into a house. The barn doors had been turned into a grand floor-to-ceiling window, and the horizontal wood slates were painted green-grey. Bright floodlights shone across the property. Since they were in the countryside and close to the motorway bridge, it was the only form of light in the area.

A little hesitant, Eddie followed the winding brick path to the front door, while Rex cut across the grass with Dave the cat in his arms. Rex pushed the doorbell. An enthusiastic, bald man with a grey moustache opened the door. He wore a flannel shirt with rolled-up sleeves, blue jeans, and leather slippers.

"Hello," he said. "You must be Dave's new friends."

"I'm home, Daddy," Rex said through his teeth, pretending to be the cat.

The man held Dave up to his chin, the cat rubbed his face into the man's cheeks.

"Thank you so much. Where did you find him?"

Eddie tilted his head. "Uh, down the street by the bridge."

"Ha, he was practically on my doorstep the whole time."

"We should get going," Eddie said.

"The reward!" The bald man smiled. "Let me grab my wallet."

Eddie raised his palm. "That's not necessary."

The man placed the cat on the ground. "Nonsense, you took care of my little fluff-ball, you deserve to get paid."

He walked back into the house.

Rex slapped Eddie's shoulder with the back of his hand. "How could you turn down the money? You told me off about going pro-bono, and now you're rejecting a cash reward."

"Because we took the cat to begin with."

"We solved the case, Eddie. We should take the money."

Eddie grunted. "I'll take it to avoid the embarrassment of explaining why we don't deserve it."

The cat sat in the doorway watching Rex and Eddie as if judging them. Expressionless really, but the eyes said, 'You kidnapped me.'

Eddie knelt down to the cat's level. "We brought you back, didn't we?"

Rex folded his arms. "So I can't speak cat, but the cat can speak English. That makes sense."

The man returned with cash in hand. "The reward was for one hundred pounds, but I only have a fifty and three twenties, so I made it one hundred and ten."

"We have change." Eddie pulled the coins from his pocket. "Well, about five pounds worth."

"Don't be silly. It's a ten-pound bonus; you deserve it."

"No, we don't," Eddie said.

"Oh, go on." The man held the wad of cash out at them.

Rex snatched the money and repeatedly counted it with glee.

"Thank you so much. What are your names?"

"Rex," Rex said. "Rex Milton and Eddie Miles. We're partners."

"Business partners," Eddie added.

"And what business is that?"

"We're private detectives," Rex said.

"Well, I never. I've not met a detective before, and now I've met two real detectives who found my cat. I thought a neighbour might find him, not a real, bona fide detective—two, no less. You're stupendous."

Rex and Eddie recoiled.

"That's a good thing," the man said. "Rex and Eddie, you will be in my prayers, and if you're not into prayer that's fine, I mean no offence. You like karma? Because I'm sure you've got some karma coming to you after the deed you did today." He smiled wide and winked. "I hope what you did comes back to you two-fold."

"Thanks!" Rex said.

"Thanks," Eddie mumbled.

As they left, the man held up Dave and shook his paw to make him wave. "Goodbye," he said from the back of his throat pretending to be the cat.

Rex waved. "Bye, Dave."

Eddie stomped back to the car with his shoulders tensely scrunched up towards his neck. Rex overtook him with a spring in his step.

"Cheer up, Eddie. We solved a case."

Eddie clenched his teeth. "He gave us a reward for returning a cat we stole." Eddie got in the car and buckled up, but then remembered Rex's car door was broken and got out.

Rex climbed across the driver seat. "Now what, Eddie?"

"We have to stop the stalker and find Nubbin before Mrs Nerdlinger finds out we stole Dave. We owe her some kind of happy ending, and we're gonna deliver."

"I like your enthusiasm, Eddie. It's like you're full of hope and that's really important. What's the plan?"

"I haven't a clue. With our track history, we're doomed to fail, and Mrs Nerdlinger is gonna have a mental breakdown when she finds out what we did."

"It'll work out."

Eddie sneered. "How?"

"If I had a penny for every time you got down, but we still made it somehow, I'd have..." Rex added up in his mind. "Twelve? Maybe fifteen pence?" He shrugged. "That's still a lot. Not in terms of pennies, but in terms of how many times things worked out."

"So you have a plan?"

Rex sighed and sat back. "How about we get her a new cat?"

"No, cats are far too difficult. They all seem to die, go missing, or live double lives."

"This is complicated," Rex said. "We can recheck the campsite?"

Rex and Eddie got out of the car and proceeded down the mud path alongside the bridge. Eddie picked up a stick to help him wade through the sludge.

The pair searched through the caravan for clues but

found nothing new. The musky smell seemed even stronger.

Rex covered his nose "Why does it smell so bad?"

"This area sometimes floods during heavy rain. With the flat tyres, I guess he couldn't move it."

They stepped outside, defeated. Eddie sat in the caravan's doorway. "This is a dead end. We've lost him."

"We can't give up, Eddie. Some weirdy-beardy catnapper is out there, and we have to stop him."

"How? He's gone, we've got no clues or anything."

Desperate to find some kind of evidence, Rex searched around. He kicked at the mud, which flung a lump into the bike tyre tracks. Rex stepped to the tracks with intense focus. Eddie raised his head from his hands.

"What is it, Rex?"

"The boy, Jeremy. What was he doing up on the mound last night?"

"I don't know. Probably wanted a good lookout."

Rex speedily trod along the tracks. Once he reached the mound, he ran. Eddie dragged himself along.

"Jackpot," Rex said.

A little out of breath, Eddie reached Rex at the top of the concrete slope. In the crevice where the mound met the top of the underpass, they found plastic tarp tucked around a rectangular shape.

Rex pulled the tarp to one side revealing a row of cardboard boxes.

"The bearded man stored stuff up here?" Eddie said. "Why?"

"To keep it dry." Rex opened the closest box. He peeked inside at random books, CDs, clothes, and camping gear. They rummaged further and found a dusty, worn-out box. It was hard to tell the dust from the general disintegration of the box.

Rex opened it but jumped back, holding his nose. "This one smells wrong."

Eddie handed Rex the stick. Rex poked at the top flap.

"Just do it," Eddie said, full of nerves.

Rex lifted open the flaps. He couldn't look inside because of the lack of light.

"It needs to be pulled out."

Eddie took a step back. "Go on then."

With his foot, Rex dragged the box forward, flipping it onto the mound. The body of a cat fell half out of the box.

Rex and Eddie both spun around screaming.

Eddie uncontrollably shook his arms. "Oh god! It's a dead cat in a box! The cat in the box is dead!"

The pair walked off the discomfort. Eddie quickly glanced at the box. He saw a paw on the concrete, but the rest of the body lay in the shadows.

"What do we do, Eddie?"

"We have to ID the cat. So we can tell Mrs Nerdlinger."

The corners of Rex's mouth drooped. "I don't want to look at it again."

"Me neither." Eddie took a deep breath. "We'll do it together."

Rex nodded.

The pair stepped with trepidation towards the box. Eddie slowed down, letting Rex get a little ahead. Rex, wise to Eddie's game, curbed his speed. Eventually, the pair slowed until they both stood-still five-feet from the cat.

Eddie rolled his eyes. "Fine." He marched towards the box and shifted it. The box felt lighter than he expected. The cat rolled out with a jingle.

"What's making that noise?" Rex said.

"The collar?"

"It's not wearing a collar."

Eddie inspected closer. The fluffy cat's hair looked perfect and clean. He grabbed the cat.

Rex jumped back, "Uh, no. Don't touch it."

"It's not a cat," Eddie said.

"What is it?"

Eddie threw it towards Rex.

Rex covered his face. "Don't throw that at me!"

"It's a cuddly toy. A stuffed animal."

Rex examined the toy cat's big, glossy eyes; its smiling mouth appeared to be laughing at them.

"He keeps a cuddly cat toy in an old box?" He shook the grey cat. The bell inside jingled. "Then what was the smell?"

Eddie checked around by the boxes until he found a half-eaten rat. "A dead rodent."

"Must've been Dave," Rex said.

"Dave?"

"Dave the cat."

Eddie rolled his eyes.

"Dave the cat!" Rex picked up the cuddly toy and shook it at Eddie. "The toy looks just like Dave."

"Well, kind of. It's a grey tabby I guess."

Rex smiled. "And Dave looks just like Professor Buttons."

Eddie raised the corner of his lip. "Professor Buttons was a toy this whole time? Mrs Nerdlinger really has lost the plot."

Eddie pulled a blanket from the box with the name Danny stitched on it.

Rex cocked his head. "Who's Danny?"

"I think we need to learn a bit more about Mrs Nerdlinger."

ELEVEN

The next morning Rex and Eddie waited down the street for Mrs Nerdlinger to leave her home. She fed her cats on the patio, locked up, and left for work. Eddie opened the car boot, and the pair pulled out a glass coffee table.

"This better work," Eddie said.

"It's the only way," Rex said. "Besides, you didn't want the reward money for Dave the cat anyway."

"Still, a hundred quid for a coffee table is a bit much."

They carried the table to Ian Stork's door and knocked. The blinds to the front window clipped open and shut.

"What do you want?" Stork called out.

"We want to ask you a few questions about Mrs Nerdlinger."

"Why should I help you?"

"There is a cat-stealing weirdo on the streets, and he might have a thing for Mrs Nerdlinger."

"We all have a thing for Beatrice," Stork replied.

"She might be in danger, you want that on your hands?"

"That's why I should help Beatrice; why should I help you?"

"A new coffee table?"

He opened the front door and smiled big enough to reveal both rows of his thin, yellow teeth. "You replaced the coffee table you broke."

"You broke it," Eddie said.

Stork turned his nose up. "Because he moved."

"When you threw a bat at me," Rex said.

"Because of a chain of events put into place when you entered my home, uninvited."

Rex and Eddie stared at each other.

"Fine," Eddie said. "It doesn't matter. Can we talk about Mrs Nerdlinger?"

Stork had them bring the coffee table into the living room. He brought out a tray of tea and biscuits and placed them on the table. He gave a joyful smile as he sat back.

"Oh that's very nice," he said. "So what is it you wanted to talk about?"

Eddie picked up his tea and sipped. "Have you seen a bearded man come to Mrs Nerdlinger's house?"

"I saw someone like that knock at her door a couple of weeks ago. It didn't cause any issues."

"You gave us a hard time."

"That was after the cat went missing and Beatrice got upset."

Rex held up the cuddly toy cat. "Do you recognise this cat?" The stuffed animal jingled as Rex plonked it next to the tea.

"Get that thing off my coffee table."

"Did she ever have a cat called Professor Buttons?" Eddie asked.

"Ever since I've known her, she's had at least one cat, I don't know their names."

"Does this toy cat remind you of one of her cats?"

"Maybe one of the early ones. It's been a few years."

Eddie leaned forward. "Who's Danny?"

Stork stroked his chin. "Danny? Daniel, you mean? Her ex-husband was Daniel Nerdlinger."

"That's the bearded man. He's tormenting her, and you did nothing?" Eddie said.

"I didn't know he was bothering her."

"You didn't recognise your old neighbour?"

"No, no. Beatrice moved next door right after the separation. She was cagey about the whole thing, but I knew his name was Daniel."

"What did he do for a living?"

"He was a teacher, I believe. Before she moved to Cloisterham, they both taught at the all-boys school out in Maidenstone."

Eddie parked the car outside the William Shipley School For Boys. "I hope this is worth it," he said. "Twelve miles each way is five litres of petrol in this old thing."

Rex and Eddie approached the school. A grand Tudor building stood at the centre with a circular brick tower down the side. Attached to the left was a sixties-style extension with large, glass windows in crumbly frames and a flat rooftop. Attached to the right was a nineties-style extension made of yellow bricks, small windows, and a sloped roof.

They stepped inside. The reception was a round room with circular alcoves containing busts of old men. Next to the head teacher's large office, a woman in her late thirties with a short bob and hoop earrings typed at her desk.

"Hello," Eddie said. "We'd like to get some information on Daniel Nerdlinger."

"He's teaching at the moment," she said without looking up from the screen.

"He still works here?" Rex asked.

She looked away from her screen and blew a bubble with her gum. "Why else would you come here?"

Eddie curled his lip. "Is that gum?"

"Yes," the receptionist said.

"Are you allowed gum?"

"What are you? A teacher?"

Rex rolled his eyes. "Chill out, Eddie. The war on gum is over."

The receptionist checked her computer. "Mr Nerdlinger is teaching."

"Can you call him?"

"You're not allowed phones."

"Just gum?"

"Are you going to tell on me?" The receptionist winked. "What do you want to see Mr Nerdlinger about?"

"It's, uh, a private matter."

She looked the pair up and down. "Wait a second, are you police officers?"

Eddie smiled. "We really shouldn't talk to you about this. This information is for Daniel Nerdlinger only."

The receptionist took out her gum.

"Of course, officer. Mr Nerdlinger is on the school field teaching football."

Rex and Eddie stepped outside toward the school field. It was a cold day with stuffy clouds. The miserable students ran around in an attempt to avoid goosebumps from the cold. The pair stood on the sidelines looking for a tall, bearded man. Aside from the students running around the field, they only saw the back of a stocky, hunched man in a red, worn tracksuit standing on the sidelines.

"Come on, you reprobates!" he shouted. "Put some bloody effort into it."

The detective duo walked up to him.

Eddie cleared his throat. "Excuse me, we're looking for Mr Nerdlinger."

The man spun around in an about-turn. He was bald except for an acute triangle tuft of grey hair above his red face. His arms and legs were chunky and muscular. Although he was in his mid-sixties, he had defined pecs above a round belly. His eyes were milky with cataracts.

"Where's your uniform?" he barked.

"Oh, well. No. We're not policemen—"

"You being smart, boy?"

Eddie panicked "No, it's just—"

"No, sir," the man said.

Eddie swallowed. "No, sir."

"You will refer to me as sir or Mr Nerdlinger. And stand up straight when you're talking to me. Can't have you moping about like those dossers outside the dole office waiting for their government handouts. Show some respect."

Eddie straightened up; his subservient side immediately emerged. This happened to Eddie so often, he was sure that if there was a subservient gene, he had it, and it was dominant.

"You can't wear your own clothes to P.E. You'll have to go to the leftover box and pick something out."

"We aren't students."

He narrowed his eyes. "How old are you?"

"Twenty-eight," Rex said with a grin.

Nerdlinger stepped into Rex's personal space. "Am I looking at you?"

"Do you mean now or then."

"You talk when you are being spoken to."

Rex's eyes darted between Eddie and Nerdlinger. "Like now?"

"Shut it."

"I think I'm being spoken to, but the words are shut up. I'm confused."

"Drop and give me ten, both of you."

Eddie winced. "But we aren't—"

"You want me to make it twenty?"

Eddie sighed and lowered into position. Rex followed. At two push-ups, although it felt like five, Eddie's hands were cold on the wet grass, but his shoulders burned. Already on push-up six, Rex continued with a smile. At five, Eddie dropped to the ground. His face splatted in the mud.

Mr Nerdlinger bent down. "Is that all you've got, you petulant little turd?"

Eddie blinked, unsure if the grey cloud above had brought rain or if Mr Nerdlinger sprayed spit as he spoke.

On push-up six, the rain thickened. By push-up eight, Eddie lost his grip on the rain-softened mud and his arms slid out.

Mr Nerdlinger sneered. "Get up."

The pair rose.

"Now, what do you want?"

"We're private detectives," Eddie said. "Are you Danny Nerdlinger?"

The man scoffed. "What's he done now?"

Eddie narrowed his eyebrows. "Pardon?"

"Danny, what's that scruffy urchin done to earn your attention?"

"I'm sorry, who's Danny?"

"Although it pains me to say it, he's my offspring."

Eddie jolted upright. "Mrs Nerdlinger has a son?"

Is that who we've been chasing? He thought. *Her son is the cat thief?*

Mr Nerdlinger gave a smile. "My ex-wife is involved, is she?"

"Do you know how we can get in touch with Danny?"

"I kicked that spineless reprobate out on his ear five-years-ago, the jobless twit had no stamina."

"That was the last time you saw him?"

"Yes. I should have known he'd go cry to his mummy. What's she up to now? I bet she's an old cat lady."

"The prettiest cat lady you ever saw," Rex said in her defence.

He glared at Rex in disapproval. "I think you best be going."

Rex and Eddie turned to the school entrance.

"Not you." He pointed at Eddie. "You still owe me push-ups!"

TWELVE

Rex and Eddie parked outside St Jude Primary School. Over the hedge, they could see Mrs Nerdlinger through the windows teaching her class with radiant energy.

"I don't like this," Rex said. "What if Mrs Nerdlinger sees us here?"

"We tell her we stole back the cat, you punched her long-lost son, and now we can't find him or Nubbin."

"Really?"

"No. We run."

Rex nodded. "Solid plan."

Mrs Nerdlinger stepped away from the window and wrote on the classroom's blackboard.

Eddie tapped Rex on the shoulder. "Go, go, go!"

The pair rushed to the school's entrance. Inside, they puffed with winded breath as the receptionist stared at them suspiciously.

"Do you want to speak to Mrs Nerdlinger?"

Eddie darted his head around to make sure she wasn't close. "No, absolutely not."

Rex shrunk with his hands out wide. "She's not here is she?"

"We need to speak to Jeremy Platt," Eddie said.

"Only parents or guardians can take out a pupil."

Rex and Eddie marched back to the car, but Eddie slowed as they passed the staff car park. From the corner of his eye, he saw the Ford Focus, fully repaired with a new headlight and new side panelling. The paint job was adequate, but a little bolder than the original paint.

Rex reached the side of the road and hid behind the hedge. Eddie stomped over to the Focus and kicked the headlight. His foot bounced off the unaffected vehicle. He clenched his jaw and tried again.

"Maybe we should leave it," Rex called out. "Things are even."

Eddie got out his keys, dragged them along the side of the Focus, and ran off the school property.

The pair approached the Morris Minor.

"Do we wait outside until the school finishes?" Rex said.

"Only if we want to end up on a list."

The school bell rang. Children rushed out of the class-rooms into the adjacent field.

Rex wandered along the hedge to the field's seven-foot chain link fence. "Hey, Jeremy! Jeremy Platt?"

"Rex, you're not meant to do that. It's frowned upon."

"Jeremy Platt!"

Eddie scampered to the fence. "Please stop."

A patrolling dinner lady watched them from the back of the field. She stepped closer with her arms folded. Rex and Eddie noticed her and pretended to examine the foliage with mock interest.

From amongst the crowd of boys and girls in matching

bold blue jumpers and grey trousers or skirts, Jeremy stepped out with a girl on his arm.

"What do you two want?"

Rex smiled. "This must be the Tracy we've heard so much about."

"We know you were up by those boxes under the bridge," Eddie said. "We've been through them, but we can't find any information. Did you take anything?"

"Why should I tell you?"

"Because if it weren't for us, you'd still be in detention right now."

"I got me out of detention. You two just slowed me down."

"Finder's fee?" Rex offered.

Eddie nodded. "Yes, a finder's fee."

Jeremy kissed Tracy on the cheek and unwrapped his arm. "Give me five minutes, babe."

She nodded and skipped off.

"I found a cool military jacket and other army stuff in a box, and I took it."

"Excuse me," Mr Jeffries shouted from down the field. "Stop right there."

The same dinner lady pointed Rex and Eddie out to Mr Jeffries.

Eddie ignored Jeffries in the corner of his eye. "What army stuff?"

"Mostly clothes."

Mr Jeffries stomped across the playground towards the fence. "No talking to strangers."

"Uniforms?" Rex asked. "What did you do with them?"

"They were too big, so I dumped them at the charity shop."

"Get away from that fence," the head teacher called out.

"Which charity shop?" Eddie turned back to the Morris Minor and then to Mr Jeffries.

"The homeless one on the high street."

Eddie nodded and scrambled to the car.

Mr Jeffries caught up enough to recognise Rex and Eddie. "The detectives?"

"Bye," Rex said.

The pair ran to the Morris Minor, and Eddie pulled out the key.

"You?" Mr Jeffries face turned red. "It was you!"

He pulled out a large ring of school keys attached to his belt and ran to the fence gate.

Eddie's car key didn't fit in the driver's door properly. Scratching up the Focus gave the key a slight bend. He gave an awkward smile and tried again.

Mr Jeffries wiggled his key until the fence unlocked and stormed out into the street.

Eddie jammed car key halfway into the lock. He used the weight of the Morris Minor to leverage bending the key straight. With a hard shove, the whole key slotted in. Eddie turned the key and opened the door. Rex climbed through the driver's side to the passenger seat.

Jeffries marched around the car to the driver's side as Eddie sat down and slammed the door. He started the car as Jeffries kicked the un-dented side.

Sensing that the Morris Minor was about to pull away, Jeffries grabbed the remaining side mirror, not realising it was actually a small shaving mirror glued to the side of the car. The mirror popped off the car into Jeffries' hand. His confused reflection stared back at him as the Morris Minor drove away.

Eddie rummaged through the charity shop clothing rack in search of the military jacket. He turned to check Rex was doing the same, but found him in front of a mirror sizing up a t-shirt with a target pattern in the centre.

"You think this suits me?"

"I don't know, Rex. Sometimes we get shot at. You sure you want to wear a bullseye?"

Rex shook his head and put the t-shirt back.

"Can you help me find the military jacket?" Eddie said, his hands shuffling through a rack as he spoke.

"Of course."

A tall man with a beard brushed past Eddie.

Danny Nerdlinger? he thought.

After staring long enough to get caught, he realised the bearded man was a hipster on the lookout for vintage clothes. In fact, there were several trendy beard types around the shop.

So hard to tell the difference between a fashionable person and a homeless person these days, he thought.

Eddie found a green camouflage jacket, but on closer examination he spotted a small German flag stitched on the side. He fingered through more clothes until he heard Rex giggle.

"Hey, Eddie. Remember these?"

Rex picked up a mounted rubber fish and pushed the button. The fish slapped its tail and sang 'Don't Worry, Be Happy.'

Eddie's shoulders hunched up. "Will you concentrate?"

Rex placed the fish back on the shelf as it continued to sing. The pair checked every clothes rack twice and didn't find the jacket.

"Useless. Completely useless." Eddie slumped into a

worn leather armchair. "At least with the jacket we might have found something, maybe identified his rank, checked the pockets for clues."

Rex stood on his tiptoes to view the heads of mannequins in the display window, their bodies covered by shelves of old VHS and cassette tapes. He ran to the front of the shop and looked out. The mannequins wore three-piece suits. Defeated, Rex moped back to Eddie. He stopped and stared over Eddie's shoulder.

"What?" Eddie slowly turned around.

At the counter sat a man in a green military jacket helping an elderly customer. The pair approached the counter from behind as the sales assistant handed the old man his change.

"Excuse me," Eddie said.

The man at the counter turned around. He had a bushy beard and a tired face.

"You two?" the man said as he stood. "What do you want from me?"

"I … um, I just wanted to ask if you got your jacket from here?"

"Why? Why won't you leave me alone?"

Eddie shuffled back. "Sorry?"

Rex lifted his fist and held it up near the man's beard. The man slapped Rex's hand away.

"Ouch," Rex blew on his knuckles.

Eddie turned to Rex, whose eyes were wide.

The man stepped out from the counter towards them, slowly and deliberately. As he approached the pair, it dawned on Eddie that this wasn't some volunteering hipster.

"You're Danny Nerdlinger."

THIRTEEN

Rex and Eddie sat on the bench in Mrs Nerdlinger's front garden. As they waited for her to return, the various cats rubbed against the pair's feet. Mrs Nerdlinger arrived wearing an orange tank top and blue denim shorts. The bold orange accentuated the light freckles across her white skin.

She greeted them on the patio with a mellow tone. "Afternoon, boys. I'm afraid Professor Buttons is gone."

Eddie shifted in his seat. "I know, but I think we can make things better. This isn't quite the cat you were expecting, but do you recognise this?"

Rex pulled the cuddly toy from his backpack.

Her forehead wrinkled. "Is that Professor Buttons?"

"Was Professor Buttons a real cat, Mrs Nerdlinger?"

"Of course."

"Then who is this?"

"It looks like the original Professor Buttons." She swallowed and took a deep breath. "My son, he had this cuddly toy, and he called it Professor Buttons. I named my first cat after the Professor."

"When did you last see your son?"

"Twenty years ago. My husband and I had a very messy divorce. He lied and said I broke my son's arm when he was three years old. They came to my home, saw my clutter, and designated me an unfit parent. My ex-husband was given full custody. I wasn't allowed near him."

Eddie solidly nodded. "The man we chased from your house the other night. He wasn't a cat thief. He's your son."

Her eyebrows pulled together. "You found Danny?"

Rex smiled wide showing his top teeth. "Danny found you, Miss."

"He's the footprint in the mud. When he learned you lived here, he visited multiple times, but every time he knocked, no one was home."

"Except for the time we broke in," Rex said.

She pulled in her chin. "You broke into my house?"

"We searched the crime scene," Eddie said. "We didn't break in."

Rex nodded. "That's true. We used the key under the plant pot."

Eddie jabbed Rex with his elbow.

She placed a hand on her chest. "You've been inside my home?"

"We're getting off topic," Eddie waved to the white van across the street.

Danny Nerdlinger stepped out of the van in clean boots, jeans, a grey shirt, and his returned military jacket. He'd kept his long beard after Rex assured him he looked trendy.

"Danny?" Mrs Nerdlinger put her hands on her heart. "Danny, is that you?"

"Mum?" Danny ran across the garden and hugged her.

As she joyfully laughed, Eddie admired the way her nose crinkled.

She examined Danny's eyes and touched his face. "It really is you. I'm sorry. I went to your father's on your eighteenth birthday, but you were gone."

"It's not your fault. He kicked me out when I was seventeen. We argued, and he broke my arm. That's when I knew he's the one who hurt me before."

Mrs Nerdlinger's eyes welled up.

"I joined the army to toughen up, but the military was more Dad than Dad."

"You were in the army this whole time?"

"I got out six months ago. I've been meeting Beatrice Nerdlingers all over the country trying to find you. I had no idea you were only twelve miles away."

"You're here now."

"Can we go inside?" he asked.

Mrs Nerdlinger winced. "I … it's a mess. I can't even live here anymore."

"She sleeps in her car," Rex said.

Eddie nudged him. "Don't be insensitive."

"What? I'm helping them find common interests."

Danny patted her on the shoulder. "I can help you tidy up. I volunteer for a charity shop, and we're always looking for donations."

She smiled. "That would be lovely."

Rex leaned into their space. "Mrs Nerdlinger, Professor Buttons, was … not the same cat."

"Oh, I know," she said.

Eddie's eyebrows raised. "You knew?"

"He's changed. I don't know what he's seen while he was away, but he came back a changed cat. He seemed happy though, and wherever Nubbin is, I'm sure she's happy, too."

Eddie turned to Rex. "That's the end for us. I guess we should go."

"Case solved!" Rex said.

"It wasn't exactly a case; we weren't hired."

Rex tiled his head. "A quest?"

Eddie sneered. "That's a bit too fanciful."

"Well, what was it then?"

"A deed," Mrs Nerdlinger said. "A good deed, done."

Rex curled his top lip, unimpressed with the minimal feat. "At least I got my special risk-taking powers from the cat."

"No, Rex. I'm not talking toxoplasma with you."

Mrs Nerdlinger sighed. "You've been listening to Ian, haven't you?"

Eddie bobbed his head while Rex nodded.

"For a human to become infected with toxoplasma gondii they would need to literally consume infected cat faeces."

The pair cringed at the idea.

"Even if you touched the excrement, as long as you wash your hands before eating, you'll be fine."

Eddie smiled with relief and turned to Rex, who bit his bottom lip with concern.

Eddie shook his head. "You're disgusting, Rex."

Mrs Nerdlinger smiled with another crinkle to her nose. She wrapped an arm around each of the detectives and hugged them tightly. Held close, they could see each other's squished up faces over her shoulder. They both eyeballed their partner, annoyed to have to share the hug.

After saying goodbye, the pair left the house and looked out onto the street, various cats at their feet.

"Shall I tell my nan to make us a victory dinner?" Rex said.

"We have something to do first."

Rex and Eddie approached Mrs Pickles's house.

"Are you sure, Eddie?"

"She should know we didn't find Nubbin, or Cleopatra, or whatever the cat's called."

"I don't think she'll appreciate it."

He tapped the door knocker.

The small woman opened her door and stared at them through her thick frames. "What do the pair of you want?"

"We came to say we didn't find your cat."

"If everyone that didn't find my cat knocked on my door, I'd have little time for anything else."

"We just wanted to let you know we didn't find her, so you didn't think the other lady had her."

"She bloody did! I want my money back."

"We weren't paid, it was reward only."

"I still think I should be compensated somehow. I should sue your client."

"I can assure you Mrs Nerdlinger didn't have Cleopatra these last couple of weeks."

"Then why did Cleopatra come home the other day with a collar and a name tag calling her Princess?"

"That wasn't our client."

"Of course it was. My Cleopatra hates collars, and she was flipping about the place until I took it off. I phoned up the number on the tag and told that woman she had a bloody cheek, taking and renaming my cat. What's her game, eh?"

"We don't know this woman," Eddie said.

"She said she went on holiday to the Seychelles, and she put my Cleopatra up in a cat hotel. A cat prison more like! What's her address?"

Eddie rolled his eyes. "I don't know, you spoke to a third owner."

Mrs Pickles turned red. "I'm the only owner."

"I don't get it," Rex said.

"This cat's been lording it up at three different homes, but her cover was blown when someone put her in a cat hotel."

Mrs Pickles folded her arms. "Cat prison!"

"What a cheek," Rex said.

"Cheek indeed, stealing my cat."

Rex curled his lip. "I meant the cat, feeding off three different people."

"My Cleopatra was a victim in all this."

The black, tailless cat approached the doorway and rubbed itself against Mrs Pickles.

"You can tell your client Cleopatra is an indoor cat now."

Rex and Eddie backed away from the door.

"Will do," Eddie said.

"What kind of pet detectives are you anyway?"

"We aren't pet detectives," Eddie shouted. "We're detectives who happened to take on a pet case, but that's the last case we'll ever do with an animal. I can assure you."

They returned to the car and Eddie unlocked the driver's door.

Rex climbed over to his seat. "What's wrong with pets?"

Eddie sat and closed the door. "Nothing, it's the owners I have trouble with."

"Time to celebrate?"

"Celebrate what? We've got no money, we failed to find the cat, we fought an old man with a heart condition, and we became cat thieves ourselves."

"Cheer up, Eddie. We sorted out a family reunion. That's impressive."

"And what do we have to show for it?"

"We should tell my Nan. She'll be proud of us."

"And?"

"And she'll probably make us a full English breakfast to celebrate."

Eddie checked the time on the dashboard. "At five pm?"

"There's never a bad time to have a full English."

Eddie nodded. "All right, off to your house for a victory breakfast … for dinner."

Rex & Eddie return in

THE OFFICE SPY

GET A FREE BOOK!

ENJOY THIS BOOK?
YOU CAN MAKE A BIG DIFFERENCE!

Book reviews are an excellent tool for getting the attention of new readers. If you've enjoyed *Feline Fatale* I would be very grateful if you could spend just five minutes leaving an honest review (it can be as short as you like) on the book's Amazon page.

Thank you very much.

ABOUT THE AUTHOR

 Sean Cameron is from Rochester, England and currently lives in Los Angeles, California. When not laughing at the British weather report, he finds time to write the comedy book series *Rex & Eddie Mysteries*.

He likes carrot cake, dinosaurs, and hiking; although not much hiking happens as he fears being eaten by a mountain lion. He dislikes squash soup, traffic, and mountain lions.

You can drop him an email at sean@sean-cameron.com or visit his online home at www.sean-cameron.com.

facebook.com/seancameronauthor

twitter.com/seancameronuk

instagram.com/seancameronuk

amazon.com/author/seancameron

ALSO BY SEAN CAMERON

Catchee Monkey: A Rex & Eddie Mystery (Book 1)

Amateur sleuths Rex and Eddie stumble upon a murder mystery that sees them outnumbered, outgunned, and outwitted. They'll have to solve the case before it kills them or before they end up killing each other. *Catchee Monkey* is a hilarious detective novella that's equal parts British Comedy and gripping thriller.

Feline Fatale: A Rex & Eddie Mystery (Book 2)

Rex and Eddie accept a case to find the missing cat of their old school teacher and first crush, Mrs Nerdlinger. The duo are pitted against a creepy stalker, a nosey neighbour, and a rude old woman claiming to be the cat's real owner. *Feline Fatale* is a fun and farcical thriller full of sharp dialogue, clever twists, and silly antics.

The Office Spy: A Rex & Eddie Mystery (Book 3)

Spies, sleuths, and sandwich thieves — For Rex and Eddie, it's just another day in the office. Hired to find a corporate spy, Rex and Eddie go undercover as pest exterminators. Their spy hunting antics entangle the pair in office politics, employee secrets, and the search for the kitchen's sandwich thief. *The Office Spy* is a fun novella packed with silly hijinks, clever jokes, and crazy thrills.

The Third Banana: A Rex & Eddie Mystery (Book 4)

After a routine surveillance job ends in witnessing a kidnapping, dimwitted detectives Rex and Eddie get on the wrong side of super sleuth Jason Cole. He's special forces, they're just… special. Now the detective duo must prove their worth against the best, solve the kidnapping case, and stop a gang turf war that could destroy their hometown. Full of witty mayhem, *The Third Banana* is a comedy thriller with appeal.

ACKNOWLEDGMENTS

I'd like to thank the following for their help with this book: Eleanor Hoal, Sam Whittam, John Atkins, and Julian Maurer.

Made in the USA
Las Vegas, NV
27 November 2021

35345251R00080